I0822263

BENEATH THE EARTH

Beneath the Earth

ISBN: 979-8-9886823-2-5 (hardback)
978-1-7378736-9-3 (paperback)

Printed in the United States of America

BENEATH THE EARTH

GARY J. ROSE

BOOK DEDICATION

In loving memory and tribute, to my beloved mother, who always took the time to be the first to read my manuscripts. Though she now resides in heaven, I know she watches over me alongside my dad, who continues to support my journey. As the role of the first reader passes on, I extend my heartfelt gratitude to my sister, Debbie Miller, whose keen eye not only catches errors but also enriches the book with suggestions that make it even more captivating.

To all my devoted Jeannie Loomis fans, I am eternally grateful for your unwavering support. Your transition to reading my first horror book, "House on Haunted Hill Resurrection," propelled it into the top 10% of its genre. I hope to keep thrilling you with my upcoming horror novels.

Reviews, like a lifeline, breathe vitality into an author's world. As an Indie writer, contrary to popular belief, book publications do not often yield substantial profits, unless one possesses an unlimited budget for promotional firms and has a massive platform and following. Instead, I rely on the kindness of my loyal fans who share my work in conversations with their friends and family.

I invite you to embark on an adventure as you delve into "Beneath the Earth," a nod to the days when Hollywood brought forth creature features that, though campy, provided us with unforgettable scares and screams during our formative years. May this book transport you to a realm of thrills and nostalgia, reminding us of the magic of storytelling that endures through generations.

FORWARD

A JOURNEY TO THE CLASSIC HORRORS OF YESTERYEARS

Welcome, dear reader, to a thrilling expedition into the realms of nostalgia and terror. In this forward, we embark on a journey that will take us back to a bygone era, a time when horror cinema was a mesmerizing blend of suspense, science fiction, and spine-chilling creatures. Let's explore the captivating realm of the 1950s and 1960s, where the silver screen was adorned with monochrome charm.

In this era, regular individuals confronted extraordinary terrors, etching an enduring legacy in the world of cinema. Special effects were a far cry from the extravagant spectacles we witness in modern Hollywood. Back then, a mere 35 cents granted you admission to the movie theater, while a refreshing soda and a bag of popcorn could be savored for a mere 15 cents. On Friday nights, a carload of moviegoers could enjoy the drive-in experience for just one dollar.

It's fascinating to revisit these classic creature features and observe the inherent campiness that often characterizes them. While some of it can be attributed to the limitations of special effects during their time, it's also true that many of these films relied on the spectacle of their monsters to compensate for weak or lacking scripts.

Indeed, despite their imperfections, these movies have managed to withstand the test of time. They possess a certain enduring quality that continues to captivate audiences, even in the face of technological advancements and evolving storytelling techniques. While their campiness and limitations may be apparent, these creature features have managed to carve out a special place in cinematic history becoming beloved classics that have left an indelible mark on the world of film.

Before I present my list of famous creature feature films, it's important to note that these are just a selection from the many thrilling movies that captivated me during my youth. Hollywood not only delighted audiences with creature films but also introduced unforgettable non-creature classics like Frankenstein, Dracula, the Wolfman, and the Invisible Man, to name a few. Now, let's delve into a compilation of creature features that left a lasting impression on generations of fans.

Creature from the Black Lagoon," this 1954 film, takes place in the lush Amazon rainforest becomes the backdrop for a gripping tale. A group of scientists embark on an expedition and unearths a perplexing being known as the Gill-man – a remarkable hybrid of human and amphibian. As the creature becomes infatuated with one of the female members of the team, it awakens a relentless reign of terror, instilling fear in the hearts of all who crossed its path.

In the 1958 film, "**The Blob,**" a quaint town becomes the setting for an extraordinary extraterrestrial phenomenon. Descending from outer space, an alien entity resembling an amoeba arrives consuming everything in its voracious path. With each victim it engulfs, the entity grows larger and more menacing. As panic grips the community, a courageous group of resourceful teenagers must rally together to devise a plan to halt the relentless expansion of the amorphous mass before it devours the entire town.

In the movie **"Them!"** (1954), the barren deserts of New Mexico witness the emergence of an extraordinary menace-a horde of enormous ants exposed to radiation. These colossal creatures unleash destruction and multiply at an alarming rate, posing a grave threat. A team comprising scientists and military personnel unite in a desperate bid to confront the insectoid onslaught, their collective survival teetering on the edge.

In the film, **"The Thing from Another World"** (1951), sometimes referred to as **"The Thing"** finds a team of scientists stationed at a secluded Artic outpost. The film's storyline concerns a United States Air Force crew and scientists who find, frozen in the Artic ice, a crashed flying saucer and a humanoid body nearby. Returning to their remote arctic research outpost with the body still in a block of ice, they are forced to defend themselves against the still alive and malevolent plant-based alien when it is accidentally thawed out.

"The War of the Worlds" (1953), brought H.G. Well's timeless novel to life, immersing us in a harrowing struggle against malicious Martians. In this adaptation, colossal tripods rise from the earth, unleashing devastating heat rays and plunging humanity into chaos. Faced with technologically superior invaders, mankind must summon the strength to resist and survive. As the interplanetary warfare unfolds, a gripping narrative of survival unfolds, capturing the resilience and determination of the human spirit in the face of overwhelming odds.

In the film **"Godzilla"** (1954), a colossal creature awakens from the ocean depths due to nuclear testing. This ancient monster takes the form of Godzilla, a fire-breathing dinosaur-like behemoth. As it unleashes its destructive rampage upon Tokyo, humanity is forced to confront this unstoppable force of nature. However, they soon realize that the true peril lies not only in the creature itself, but also in mankind's insatiable quest for power. "Godzilla" served as a cautionary tale, reminding us of the consequences of our relentless pursuit of destructive capabilities and the need to reckon with the consequences of our actions.

While **"King Kong"** (1933), slightly predates the intended time period, its impact on the monster genre remains undeniable. Most like "Godzilla," Hollywood loves to produce sequel after sequel. The story follows the colossal creature known as King Kong, a gigantic ape residing on a mysterious island. Captured and brought to civilization as a spectacle, chaos erupts when he breaks free from captivity. Unleashing destruction in his path, King Kong embarks on a relentless rampage. Ultimately, his tragic fate leads him to find solace atop the iconic Empire State Building. "King Kong" is a timeless tale of beauty and the beast, leaving an indelible mark on the genre of monster movies and captivating audiences for generations.

In the film **"Rodan"** (1956), the aftermath of a volcanic eruption triggers the awakening of two colossal pterosaurs named Rodan from their prehistoric hibernation. Taking flight, these winged behemoths generate destructive winds that can topple buildings and unleash widespread devastation. Faced with the imminent threat of total annihilation, humanity must rally together to confront these massive airborne creatures. The survival of the human race hinges upon their ability to devise a plan and stand united against the menacing threat of Rodan.

"Mothra", (1961) is a Japanese film and a prominent character in the Toho tokusatsu films, and has made multiple appearances, frequently as a recurring figure in the Godzilla franchise. This colossal creature is typically portrayed as a sentient larva (caterpillar) or imago (adult form) and is accompanied by two miniature fairies who speak on her behalf. Unlike many other monsters in the Toho universe, Mothra is often depicted as a heroic figure, with her allegiance directed towards the protection of her own island culture, the Earth itself, and even Japan.

"The Day the Earth Stood Still" (1951), presents a captivating science fiction narrative that prompts deep contemplation. A humanoid alien named Klaatu arrives on Earth, accompanied by his formidable robot companion, Gort, bearing an urgent message for humanity. Despite Klaatu's peaceful motives, he encounters hostility and suspicion from military and government figures. As global tensions escalate, pushing the world to the precipice of self-destruction, Klaatu faces the formidable task of conveying his message of peace and awakening humanity to the dire consequences of their violent and self-destructive behavior. This thought-provoking masterpiece delves into themes of diplomacy, human nature, and the potential for redemption in the face of imminent catastrophe.

"Black Scorpion", (1957) unfolds in the desolate expanse of Mexico, weaving a gripping narrative of ancient legends and monstrous entities. A string of enigmatic deaths and vanishings sets the stage for a relentless detective, drawn into a world of supernatural phenomena. As his investigation deepens, he unravels a hidden realm governed by a malevolent sorcerer who has awakened a colossal scorpion-like creature from its dormant state. With the creature unleashing chaos and destruction upon the land, the determined detective must gather his courage and face this wicked force head-on. In this atmospheric tale, the battle between good and evil reaches its zenith amidst the eerie backdrop of Mexican folklore and dark enchantments.

In the film **"Tarantula"** (1955), a brilliant scientist seeks to solve the world's growing hunger crisis by developing a revolutionary nutrient capable of supporting the rapidly expanding human population. However, in its experimental stage, the nutrient triggers an alarming side effect – extraordinary and uncontrollable growth. The situation takes a perilous turn when a tarantula, a test subject for the nutrient, manages to escape and begins to undergo an accelerated growth process. With each passing moment, the tarantula grows larger and more menacing, posing a grave threat to all in its path. As panic ensues, the scientist must race against time to find a way to contain the oversized arachnid before it unleashes devastation on an unprecedented scale.

"The Tingler" (1959), delves into the intriguing narrative of a scientist named Dr. Warren Chapin who makes a groundbreaking discovery-a parasitic creature known as a "tingler" that resides within human beings. This peculiar organism earned its name due to its ability to make its host's spine "tingle" when experiencing fear. Dr. Chapin, a pathologist, investigates further and unveils that this tingling sensation during extreme fear is caused by the growth of the tingler creature to the human spine. The creature feeds and becomes stronger when its host is frightened, posing a danger of eventually crushing the person's spine if left curled up for too long. However, Dr. Chapin also learns that the host can weaken the tingler and prevent its curling by screaming. This suspenseful tale explores the eerie relationship between fear, survival, and the mysterious tingler parasite, challenging the boundaries of human understanding and resilience.

In the film, **"Attack of the Crab Monsters"** (1957), a team of scientists accompanied by a group of five sailors, venture onto a secluded island in the vast Pacific Ocean. Their mission is two-fold: to locate a previous expedition that vanished mysteriously and to study the consequences of radiation from nuclear tests at the Bikini Atoll on the island's flora and fauna. As they delve deeper into their research, they soon discover that the island harbors a terrifying secret. Enormous crab-like creatures, mutated and driven by insatiable hunger, begin to stalk the group, picking them off one by one. The scientists and sailors must find a way to survive this harrowing ordeal while unraveling the mysteries of the island and its monstrous inhabitants.

The film weaves a tale of suspense and survival against a backdrop of radioactive mutation, as the characters grapple with the unfathomable terrors that lurk on the island.

"The Beast from 20,000 Fathoms" was released in 1953, transporting us to the frigid reaches of the Arctic Circle. It all begins with the nuclear bomb test called "Operation Experiment," which unleashes unimaginable consequences. The detonation rouses a fearsome creature from its icy slumber-a Rhedosaurus, a carnivorous dinosaur measuring a staggering 200 feet (61 meters) in length. Held in suspended animation for millions of years, the creature is now free. Nisbitt, the sole witness to its awakening, struggles to convince others, despite being dismissed as delirious due to his state of mind during the sighting. Undeterred, Nesbitt persists in his claims and steadfast in his conviction of what he witnessed.

The awakened dinosaur embarks on a destructive journey, making its way down the eastern coast of North America. The creature's terrifying path of devastation leaves communities in turmoil and authorities scrambling for a solution. "The Beast from 20,000 Fathoms" not only captivated audiences but also served as a significant inspiration for subsequent creature features, leaving an indelible mark on the genre and directly influencing the creation of the iconic Godzilla franchise.

"Day of the Triffids," is a 1963 British horror film in which the world is devastated by a meteor shower where most people are left blind while the triffid plant spores bring horrifying animated creatures to life. Bill Masen, a merchant navy officer who was in the hospital with his eyes bandaged, and Susan, an orphaned schoolgirl who escaped unharmed, join forces. They commandeer an abandoned car to reach Bill's ship but encounter a terrifying triffid ambush along the way. Meanwhile, scientist Tom Goodwin and his wife Karen, isolated in a lighthouse, discover the perilous presence of triffids. As they struggle to survive, these disparate individuals face the daunting challenges of a world engulfed in darkness and overrun by deadly adversaries.

Building upon the traditions of these iconic films, we now venture forth into uncharted territory—a tale entitled "Beneath the Earth." In this chilling novel, we shall witness the timeless battle between man and creature, as an intrepid protagonist faces an unimaginable terror lurking beneath the earth's surface. Brace yourself for heart-pounding suspense, jaw-dropping revelations, and a rollercoaster ride of fear reminiscent of the classic horrors of yesteryears.

These additions to our exploration of classic horror and creature films further illustrate the wide range of fantastical creatures that captured the imaginations of audiences during the 1950s and 1960s. Just like the films that came before it, "Beneath the Earth" will continue the tradition of pitting man against unimaginable creatures, taking inspiration from these iconic giants of the silver screen. There may be a little campiness included also.

Get ready to witness the epic confrontation of giants, the awe-inspiring clashes, and the nail-biting anticipation that lies within the captivating narrative of "Beneath the Earth." Brace yourself as our courageous main characters confront a primordial malevolence lurking beneath the depths of the planet-a perilous entity that looms, poised to unleash havoc and devastation upon our world. Only through the united strength of the armed forces from both the United States and Russia can this terror be ended.

KOLA SUPERDEEP BOREHOLE 1995

In the dimly lit underground facility, the cacophony of noise generated by the diligent scientists and the rumbling drilling equipment was nearly unbearable. Illuminated by sporadic Russian signs cautioning all to proceed with care, tension hung in the air like a heavy fog.

Within the facility, scientists attentively monitored numerous screens displaying crucial data from the ongoing drilling operation. The atmosphere was thick with anticipation and apprehension. Slowly but steadily, a colossal drill bit carved its way through the unforgiving layers of the Earth's crust, a testament to humanity's unwavering thirst for exploration. Beads of sweat trickled down the determined faces of the workers as they toiled relentlessly, pushing the boundaries of what was deemed possible.

Their collective efforts were on the verge of triumph, as they approached a documented depth of 12,262 meters (40,230 ft). However, the control room abruptly erupted into chaos, engulfed by blaring alarms and flashing red lights. Frantically, scientists scrambled to make sense of the situation, their faces etched with concern. Panic pervaded the environment, causing people to collide in their haste and confusion.

Amidst the tumultuous chaos, the underground facility was struck by an unforeseen phenomenon. As if mimicking seismic waves, violent tremors shook the very foundations of the structure, causing the scientists to stumble and cling desperately to any stable surface within reach. Yet, these tremors were accompanied by a bone-chilling cacophony—the unmistakable clicking of mandibles and piercing shrills that echoed through the air.

Only a select few scientists possessed knowledge of this enigmatic entity lurking beneath the surface. They knew of the nameless horror that dwelled deep within the Earth, an ancient terror unknown to the rest of the world. Now, as the chaos unfolded, the dreadful truth manifested itself through the haunting sounds reverberating from the unseen depths.

Amidst the disarray, a command was swiftly issued—a harrowing directive to evacuate the site. Understanding the urgency of the situation, the scientists acted with haste. A massive metal plate, sturdy and impenetrable, was swiftly brought forth and securely fastened over the borehole. It stood as a barrier, a final defense against the sinister forces stirring below.

With the metal plate firmly in place, the order to abandon the facility resonated through the panicked atmosphere. The scientists, gripped by a mix of fear and urgency, made their way to safety, leaving behind the mysterious unknown that had unleashed chaos upon them. The eerie symphony of clicking mandibles and shrill cries faded into the distance as they retreated from the site, leaving the mysterious "thing" to remain imprisoned, hidden beneath the secured plate—a menacing secret that would continue to haunt their thoughts.

KOLA SUPERDEEP BOREHOLE - PRESENT DAY

An unsettling silence now permeated the once-bustling facility. Equipment, once vital and industrious, now lay discarded and forgotten, buried beneath layers of snow and neglect. The passage of time had etched its mark upon the abandoned machinery, leaving a haunting aura of desolation in its wake.

The borehole, a gateway into the depths of the Earth, stood before them, sealed tight with a weathered 10-inch rusted cap. Its metal surface bore witness to years of exposure to the elements, stained and corroded by the passage of time. The once-vibrant symbol of exploration now stood as a testament to the quiet stillness that enveloped the facility.

From the north, the relentless wind howled, carrying with it an icy chill that bit through any exposed flesh. The temperature, plummeting to subzero levels, created an inhospitable environment, as if nature itself sought to shroud the site in an impenetrable veil of cold indifference.

Amidst the frozen landscape, a faded sign near the borehole managed to cling to a semblance of its former glory. Its weathered surface proudly boasted of the awe-inspiring achievement accomplished many years ago, a testament to the tenacity and ambition of those who had ventured into the depths. “Kola Superdeep Borehole - Deepest Manmade Hole on Earth. 40,230 feet into the Earth’s crust.” Yet, now it served as a somber reminder of the passage of time and the fleeting nature of human endeavors.

As the wind whispered through the abandoned facility, it carried echoes of a forgotten legacy, a story left untold. The borehole, once a portal to the unknown, now stood as a solemn sentinel, silently guarding the secrets that lay dormant beneath the frozen earth.

A beat-up van drives down a snow-covered road in the Kola Peninsula, deep in the Arctic Circle. The sun is setting, casting an eerie glow. Inside the van, two Russian inspectors, Andrii and Viktor, wearing blue coveralls and orange reflective vests, listen to a Russian rock song on the radio.

Andrii unzips his coveralls and pulls out a small bottle of vodka. With one hand on the wheel, he skillfully maneuvers the van through the treacherous road. "Here. You want a drink to keep warm? This damn heater is the shits." He hands the bottle to Viktor, who takes a swig and hands it back.

"Every week we freeze our asses off driving out here and look at a fuckin hole in the ground. What does headquarters think, the Americans might steal it?" Viktor says not expecting an answer.

"What are you bitching about? Maybe you want to join the army and Putin can send you to Ukraine and get your ass shot off," Andrii replies.

"I think I am too old," Viktor replies. "Besides, didn't he say we would win the war in a month." They both laugh, their laughter echoing in the desolate surroundings.

Andrii parks the van near a crumbling building. They step out and take in the natural beauty of the lakes, forests, and mist that surround the ruins of the Kola Peninsula research station.

"Well, here we are. The beauty of nature mixed with the remnants of Soviet science," Andrii says while looking around the area.

"Yeah, in a race against the Americans to see who can get to the center of the Earth first," Viktor states. They both laugh and walk towards the center of the complex. There, they find a heavy, rusty metal cap embedded in the concrete floor, secured by a ring of thick and equally rusty metal bolts.

"Okay, as we both knew, the damn hole is still here, so let's get out of here," Viktor said, as he shook from the cold.

"Wait, asshole. We must take pictures and send them to headquarters. You want to get paid, don't you? Go get the phone and a flashlight. It's starting to get dark," as Andrii stares at the hole, Viktor returns with a flashlight and iPhone. Suddenly, a loud boom shakes the area, and the metal bolts and cap fly high in the air.

"What the hell was that?" a startled Viktor asked.

"Stop! Don't move. It might be a gas back up. We could have an explosion," Andrii said looking at the borehole. Viktor stayed close to the van and they both waited. The large hole is completely exposed.

"What's that sound? It's coming from the hole," Andrii asks.

"I don't hear anything. I say we takes pictures showing the damn cap is fucked up and get out of here. This place gives me the creeps," Viktor says.

"Shut up! Listen. That sound is getting stronger. Come closer," Adrii says as he starts walking towards the hole in the ground. Viktor starts walking in his direction.

"You know what it sounds like? It sounds like crabs when they are walking on something other than sand," Adrii says, straining to hear the sound.

"You're right," Viktor says. "It does sound like crabs walking but how in the hell would crabs get into the shaft? Fuck it. Give me the camera and focus a beam of light over the hole."

Andrii walks closer to the hole and Viktor points the flashlight down into it. Suddenly, a massive spider-like creature with sharp legs shoots out of the hole, causing Andrii to stumble backward in shock.

"Let's get the fuck out of here," Viktor shouts. The spider spews a liquid onto Viktor's face and upper body instantly burning his skin down to the bone. He screams but the creature spews even more acid on him.

Andrii runs back to the van. More and more spiders climb out of the hole emitting a vibrating purring sound. Andrii climbs into the van and locks the door. The spiders' tarsus and claws rip through the sheet metal of the van. One spider pulls Andrii from the van and after biting him, wraps him in silk, waiting for him to die, then begins to eat.

DUKE UNIVERSITY

Dr. Emily Williams, a brilliant geologist in her mid-thirties, commanded the attention of her male graduate students as she approached the podium. With her long black hair cascading down her shoulders and dressed in a sharp dark blue business suit, she exuded both intellect and elegance. A pair of reading glasses dangled from a chain around her neck, a testament to her dedication to the pursuit of knowledge.

Once she reached the podium, Dr. Williams took a moment to arrange her notes before addressing the class. The room fell into a hushed anticipation as all eyes focused on her. "Good morning," she began, her voice confident and engaging. She heard a cell phone go off and just stared at her audience who got her silent message.

"Today we have the pleasure of delving into two of my absolute favorite subjects—the Kola Superdeep Borehole and the Project Mohole dig sites." She taps on a key of her laptop and several pictures are displayed on the large screen behind her. The students leaned forward their interest piqued by Dr. Williams' enthusiasm.

"These two remarkable endeavors have shaped our understanding of the Earth's depths and have pushed the boundaries of scientific exploration," Dr. Williams continued, a warm smile gracing her face. "They represent milestones in our quest to unravel the mysteries hidden beneath the crust." Moving gracefully across the stage, Dr. Williams ignited the room with her passion for the topics at hand. Her males students just like to admire her walk.

"The Kola Superdeep Borehole stands as a testament to human ambition," she explained, her gestures emphasizing the depth and significance of the project. "It delved into the Earth's crust like no other before it, revealing astounding geological discoveries that challenged our preconceived notions and opened doors to new realms of knowledge." The students furiously jotted down notes, captivated by Dr. Williams' words.

"And then we have the legendary Project Mohole," Dr. Williams continued, her eyes sparkling with excitement. "An audacious attempt to penetrate the Earth's oceanic crust, it embodied the ambition as deep as the trenches it sought to explore. Despite facing numerous challenges and ultimately meeting an untimely end, it remains an inspiration for daring scientific pursuits."

"This, you will learn, was the United States answer to the former Soviet Union's attempt to dig deeper into the Earths' crust. Throughout this course, we will dive into the scientific triumphs, the setbacks, and the extraordinary discoveries made at these groundbreaking sites," she proclaimed, her voice filled with anticipation. "My hope is to ignite your curiosity and passion for understanding our planet's hidden secrets." A wave of enthusiasm rippled through the students, eager to embark on this journey with Dr. Williams as their guide.

"So, let us embark on this journey together," Dr. Williams concluded, her gaze encompassing the room. "Are you ready?" Not expecting an answer, Dr. Williams takes a sip of water from her water bottle and starts her lecture.

"In the early 1960s, amidst the backdrop of the Cold War, two countries, the United States and the Soviet Union set their sights on a shared objective—to drill deep into the Earth's crust. The race to plumb the depths of our planet's secrets was on, each nation propelled by a desire for scientific advancement and a quest for supremacy. The Soviets named their audacious endeavor the Kola Superdeep Borehole, a project that would captivate the world and rewrite the record books."

"On the fateful day of May 24, 1970, the drilling commenced, marking the beginning of an extraordinary journey into the unknown." As the monumental task unfolded, the students seated before Dr. Emily Williams in the lecture hall watched with rapt attention. Slide after slide projected onto the screen, showcasing captivating photographs of the awe-inspiring Kola Superdeep Borehole.

"This is what the borehole looks like today,"
She advances a slide.

"And this slide shows the whole site to give you a perspective of the area."

The students, engrossed in the lecture, absorbed the magnitude of the endeavor. Small talk breaks out between students which Dr. Williams allowed since it showed their engagement.

Each image captured the magnitude of the colossal drilling operation, the intricate machinery, and the resolute faces of the scientists who embarked on this daring feat of exploration. The photographs revealed the sheer scale of the project, illustrating the relentless drive to push the boundaries of human achievement. Dr. Williams's voice resonated with enthusiasm as she guided the students through the captivating visuals.

"These images," she explained, her words tinged with a sense of wonder, "offer us a glimpse into the magnitude of the Kola Superdeep Borehole—the deepest man-made hole in history."

"Year after year, they persevered, drilling deeper and deeper into the Earth's crust," Dr. Williams continued. "Their goal was ambitious—to uncover the mysteries buried beneath our feet and expand our understanding of the planet we call home."

As each slide advanced, showcasing the remarkable progress of the Kola Superdeep Borehole, the students' fascination grew. The photographs painted a vivid picture of the tireless efforts, the technical challenges overcome, and the triumphs achieved in the quest for knowledge.

"The Kola Superdeep Borehole surpassed all expectations," Dr. Williams stated, her voice filled with admiration. "In 1979, it achieved a staggering depth of 12,262 meters, equivalent to 40,230 feet, becoming a testament to human perseverance and scientific prowess." The lecture hall resonated with a sense of awe and inspiration. The students, immersed in the lecture, had their minds transported to a time when humanity dared to challenge the very depths of the Earth.

As the last slide faded, leaving a fleeting image of the Kola Superdeep Borehole imprinted in their minds, the students exchanged glances, their curiosity sparked, and their hunger for knowledge ignited. Dr. Emily Williams continued on.

"In terms of true vertical depth, it remains the deepest borehole in the world. It actually consisted of several boreholes. The first hole reached 11,662 meters or 30,261 feet and the second hole was started in January 1983 and reached a depth of 38,500 feet. In 1983, the drill passed 12,000 meters or 39,000 feet in the second hole, and drilling was stopped for about a year for numerous scientific and celebratory visits to the site."

Dr. Williams stops to take another sip of water before continuing. The third hole reached 12,262 meters or 40,230 feet in 1989. By the end of 1993 it broke 15,000 meters or 49,000 feet. Drilling was stopped in August 1995.

Sally, one of Dr. Williams most attentive students', raises her hand. "Dr. Williams, I think all of us are waiting to hear if any creatures were found at the Kola dig site."

"All in good time, Sally. During the drilling process, unexpectedly no basaltic layers were found at any depth in the borehole. Prior to that, geological information about the earth's crust was mostly based on analyzing seismic waves that indicated discontinuity. Scientific models had previously suggested basalt should be seen.

"Instead, the actual geological evidence from the borehole revealed there were more granites, and at much greater depths than scientists had considered. In addition to this, water was unexpectedly found at three to six kilometers, 1.8-3.8 miles deep. Water was not naturally vaporizing at any depth in the borehole. Instead, water was found at these greater depths. Scientific models previously had not predicted water to be found at such great depths." The screen displayed a report by the Soviets upon conclusion of their dig.

"The most interesting find was microscopic plankton fossils found 3.7 miles below the surface. Another unexpected discovery was a large quantity of hydrogen gas. The drilling mud that flowed out of the hole was described as "boiling" with hydrogen. Kola illustrated that certainty from a distance is no certainty at all, and a few scientific theories were left in ruin. Every time we drill a hole we find the unexpected. That's exciting, but disturbing."

A male student, whose name Dr. Williams could not recall, raises his hand. "Dr. Williams. Have you seen the Russian movie *Superdeep,* and if so, how factual do you think it is?" Laughter erupted among the students in the lecture hall, while the rest of the crowd filled the air with oohs and aahs of amusement.

"I did see that movie. That's the one that had Mutant Cordyceps as the antagonist, right?" She did not wait for an answer. "I find it highly unlikely that creatures can exist at that depth. "Yet," she paused, "another unexpected find were 24 distinct species of plankton microfossils found 4 miles deep, and they were discovered to have carbon and nitrogen coverings rather than the typical limestone or silica. Despite the harsh environment of heat and pressure, the microscopic remains were remarkably intact." She glances at her watch. "Okay, let's take a 15-minute break and we will move on to the Mohole Project."

She checked her cellphone and saw several missed calls from an unknown area code. She noticed several voice messages but decides to return the calls after she finishes her lecture. Those students who left the lecture hall started to return to their seats and Dr. Williams prepared to continue her lecture.

"Let's turn our attention to Project Mohole, the U.S. attempt in the early 1960s to drill through the Earth's crust and obtain samples of the boundary between the Earth's crust and mantle and beat the Soviets." She glanced down at her laptop to make sure that her slides of Project Mohole were ready to be displayed.

"Project Mohole was an attempt in the early 1960s to drill through the Earth's crust to obtain samples of the Mohorovičić discontinuity, or Moho, the boundary between the Earth's crust and mantle. The project was intended to provide an earth science complement to the high-profile Space Race."

As Dr. Emily Williams continued her lecture, her words filling the lecture hall with knowledge, three individuals clad in black suits entered the room. The sudden arrival of these figures caught the attention of the students, their curiosity piqued. A sense of slight perturbation settled upon Dr. Williams as she noticed the presence of the newcomers. She directed her gaze towards the female among them, sensing an air of authority surrounding her.

"Excuse me," Dr. Williams interjected, her voice firm yet polite. "Can I help you? I'm right in the middle of my lecture." The students watched in anticipation, their attention now divided between the cryptic newcomers and their esteemed professor.

The female agent raised a badge, revealing her official identification. "You are Dr. Emily Williams?" she asked, her voice steady and authoritative. Dr. Williams, though attempting to maintain her composure, felt a surge of mixed emotions—temper and nerves mingling within her. She looked directly at the agent, her eyes filled with curiosity and a hint of apprehension.

"I am," Dr. Williams replied, her voice betraying a touch of nervousness. "And you are?" she inquired, her desire for clarity palpable.

"I'm Agent Castle with the FBI. Dr. Williams, you need to come with us immediately. Please gather up your stuff." Dr. Emily Williams stood her ground, a determined look in her eyes, as she addressed the female agent who held up her badge.

"I'm sorry, but I'm not going anywhere until you tell me what this is all about," Dr. Williams declared, her voice tinged with a mix of defiance and curiosity. The female agent, aware of the urgency surrounding their mission, responded firmly but with a hint of empathy.

"We will inform you while we are underway," Agent Castle explained, her voice carrying a sense of urgency. "Time is of the essence. Please, trust that we have a pressing need for your cooperation." Dr.

Williams hesitated for a moment, her mind racing with questions and concerns. Yet, she recognized the seriousness of the situation and the necessity to act swiftly. Reluctantly, she nodded, a glimmer of trust emerging in her eyes.

"Alright," Dr. Williams consented, her voice determined. "But I expect full disclosure as soon as possible."

Dr. Williams collects her belongings and addresses her students, "Apologies, but today's class will be ending early. I'll see you all next week." Emily is guided towards a waiting black SUV. As soon as she takes her seat, she faces Agent Castle and asks, "Can you please inform me of our destination and provide some context for all of this?"

""Doctor," the agent spoke, her voice laced with urgency, "I can only disclose that this is an incredibly classified mission. Even the three of us have been kept in the dark about the circumstances that compelled us to whisk you away to the airport."

Dr. Williams felt a knot form in her stomach as she contemplated the implications. "The airport? But my daughter will be returning from school later this afternoon. I need to be there for her, to ensure her well-being."

"Dr. Williams, we've made arrangements for your neighbor, Mrs. Angelo, to look after your daughter until your return. I understand the inconvenience this imposes, but we're merely fulfilling our duty."

They arrive at the Raleigh-Durham International Airport and drove to a hangar at the far end of the tarmac. As Dr. Williams stepped into the hangar, her eyes scanned the surroundings, taking note of several individuals gathered there. Among them, her gaze locked onto a figure she instantly recognized—Dr. Emma Carter.

Dr. Carter, a seasoned geologist with her gray hair neatly tied in a bun, spotted Dr. Williams and hastened toward her with purposeful strides. She gave Emily a hug. "Emily, thank goodness I found someone familiar. Do you have any idea what on earth is happening?" her voice filled with a mix of relief and confusion.

"I wish I did," Emily replied, returning Dr. Carter's embrace. They held onto each other for a moment, seeking solace in their shared familiarity amidst the unsettling situation.

Breaking the hug, Dr. Carter's expression remained serious as she continued, "I was in my office, engrossed in working on a new paper about my recent expedition to Mount Vesuvius, when two FBI agents barged in and insisted that I accompany them. What about you?"

"Same here. I was right in the middle of delivering a lecture at the university when three agents approached me, demanding that I leave immediately. And now, here we are," Emily explained, her tone tinged with bewilderment and a touch of apprehension. She looks at the other people in the hanger. "Do you recognize any of these other people?"

"Actually, I do," Dr. Carter responded, pointing towards a figure with a substantial black beard and mustache. "That person over there is Dr. Samuel Rosner. He's a volcanologist like me." Dr. Williams followed Dr. Carter as they navigated through the crowd of people, eventually reaching Dr. Rosner. "Dr. Rosner, do you have any inkling as to why we've been brought here?" Dr. Carter inquired, her voice laced with curiosity.

Turning towards them, Dr. Rosner greeted Dr. Carter with a nod. "Hello, Dr. Carter. I'm just as clueless as you are. They brought me here about an hour ago, and I've been going around, introducing myself and trying to gather any information about what's happening. The only consensus I've gathered so far is that everyone here is a scientist," he explained, his tone reflecting a mix of confusion and intrigue. Then, he extended his hand towards Dr. Williams. "Hello, I'm Dr. Samuel Rosner."

"Hello, I'm Dr. Emily Williams. Nice to meet you," Dr. Rosner greeted warmly in response to Dr. Williams' introduction.

Dr. Carter, intrigued by the diverse assembly of scientists, inquired further. "Samuel, can you tell us about the other scientists present?"

Dr. Rosner paused, taking a moment to consider the peculiar mix of scientific disciplines represented in the gathering. "It's quite unusual indeed. We have geologists, mining experts, marine biologists, zoologists, and there's even an arachnologist among us," he replied, his voice tinged with a sense of wonder and intrigue.

Dr. Carter raised an eyebrow, her curiosity raised by the eclectic mix of scientific disciplines present. "Indeed, it is a rather peculiar combination of scientific fields," she replied, her gaze sweeping across the gathered group as she continued to observe them intently. The assortment of expertise assembled in the hangar only deepened the mystery of their purpose and the nature of the impending mission.

Dr. Williams interjected, voicing her curiosity. "I can understand the potential overlaps between certain disciplines like geology, volcanology, and even mining. They all have connections to the Earth's structure and resources. However, the inclusion of arachnology seems rather intriguing. I wonder what significance it holds in relation to our current situation."

"Agreed," Dr. Rosner said. "And don't overlook the large presence of military personnel." The crowd of scientists were escorted to a Boeing CH-47 Chinook helicopter that had been warming up on the tarmac. Inside the large helicopter the three doctors sat together glancing at the other passengers, plus heavily armed military personnel in the rear. Dr. Rosner reached across the aisle and introduced himself to a bookish looking male offering a handshake.

"Hello, I'm Dr. Rosner." He offers a handshake.

"Hello, I'm Dr. Stevenson, reciprocating the handshake.

"Any idea why we have all been summoned together?" Dr. Rosner asked.

"I'm afraid I have no idea why we are here or where we're being taken." As they exchanged pleasantries, the uncertainty surrounding their destination only deepened. Dr. Rosner, Dr. Stevenson, and the other scientists found themselves in a state of anticipation, eagerly seeking answers to the questions that lingered in their minds. Doctors Williams and Carter joined the two.

Dr. Rosner took a moment to introduce his fellow colleagues. "Allow me to introduce Dr. Carter and Dr. Williams. Dr. Carter, like myself, is a volcanologist, and Dr. Williams is a professor of geology at Duke University. We were just discussing the intriguing mix of scientific disciplines present here, and we heard that you specialize in arachnology." Dr. Carter nodded, acknowledging the introduction, while Dr. Williams looked on with curiosity.

"Yes, it's fascinating to see how your field of study blends into the broader spectrum of disciplines represented in this group," Dr. Williams added, her interest piqued. They were eager to understand the connections and potential intersections between their respective areas of expertise and the mysterious mission ahead.

Dr. Stevenson nodded in agreement. "Indeed, it is quite perplexing. It appears that all of us have been deliberately kept in the dark regarding the purpose of our gathering and the destination we are headed towards."

The deafening noise of the helicopter blades drowned out any immediate response from Dr. Rosner, Dr. Carter, and Dr. Williams. Just as they tried to communicate, a voice, belonging to an unknown female, emerged from the speakers, cutting through the clamor of the aircraft.

"Ladies and gentlemen, I apologize for the abrupt disruption to your previous engagements. Rest assured that once we touch down, a comprehensive briefing will be provided, shedding light on the incidents that necessitated your unique expertise. For now, I kindly request you to find as much comfort as possible amidst the circumstances. We anticipate reaching our destination in approximately 45 minutes. Thank you for your understanding."

With the announcement delivered, a sense of anticipation and curiosity hung in the air as the helicopter continued its journey, carrying the group of scientists towards an unknown destination, their minds filled with questions about the impending mission that awaited them.

Dr. Rosner, his curiosity getting the best of him after the announcement and armed with his knowledge of time and distance, swiftly glanced at his wristwatch. "If my calculations are correct, and taking into account our departure time, a 45-minute radius would potentially bring us to Washington D.C. or somewhere in Florida," he mused, sharing his deduction with the three other doctors.

The possibility of their destination being one of these locations added another layer of intrigue and speculation to their already unknown mission. Their minds buzzed with anticipation as they tried to piece together the puzzle, eagerly awaiting the forthcoming briefing that promised to provide answers to their burning questions.

Dr. Emily Williams, joining in the conversation and reflecting on Dr. Rosner's deductions, chimed in with her thoughts. "Considering the nature of our situation, it seems highly unlikely that we're being whisked away for a Florida vacation. Therefore, Washington D.C. appears to be the most probable destination," she reasoned, her voice laced with a mix of curiosity and anticipation.

In the Washington D.C. hangar, as dusk settled in, Drs. Williams, Rosner, Carter, and Stevenson followed the crowd as they disembarked the aircraft. Inside the hangar, they found seats arranged in front of a long table. Taking their respective seats, they observed three high-ranking U.S. Army officers and two individuals dressed in black suits joining them at the long table. However, one female in the group stood in front of a podium, drawing the attention of Dr. Williams. She abruptly left the podium approaching Dr. Williams and extended a hand in introduction.

"Dr. Williams, I'm Judith Patterson, Deputy Director of the National Security Agency" she said, her voice carrying a tone of authority mixed with professionalism. She extended her hand.

"Hello, Ms. Patterson," Dr. Williams greeted, reciprocating the handshake. Taking note of Ms. Patterson's appearance, Dr. Williams observed her slim frame and estimated her to be in her fifties, with black hair showing traces of gray. The title of Deputy

Director of the National Security Agency carried weight and added to the intrigue surrounding their mission.

"I want to express my gratitude for your presence," Patterson stated, acknowledging their attendance.

Dr. Williams, sensing the underlying tone, responded with a touch of skepticism. "I suppose I didn't really have much of a choice, did I?" she remarked, the question lingering in the air. However, Patterson maintained her stern and businesslike demeanor, opting not to respond directly.

Dr. Patterson redirected the conversation, focusing on Dr. Williams' expertise. "Dr. Williams, I'm aware of your extensive knowledge regarding both the Kola Superdeep Borehole and Project Mohole," she stated, her tone serious.

Dr. Williams nodded, confirming her familiarity with the sites mentioned. Concerned, she posed a question, "Has there been a problem at either location? Is that why you've gathered us here?" A weighty pause hung in the air as Dr. Patterson considered her words carefully, her expression reflecting the gravity of the situation.

"We find ourselves in an unprecedented situation," Patterson began, her tone conveying the seriousness of the matter. "Recent developments at the Kola Superdeep Borehole have presented us with a significant challenge—one that necessitates your expertise and insights." Dr. Williams leaned forward.

Her curiosity raised by the mention of significant developments at the site.

Patterson took a moment to collect her thoughts before responding to Dr. Williams' inquiries. "The challenge we face revolves around recent seismic activity in the vicinity of the Kola Superdeep Borehole," she explained, her voice tinged with concern. "Our investigations have led us to believe that this seismic activity is connected to an anomaly located deep within the Earth's crust. The Russian government has requested our assistance."

Dr. Williams furrowed her brow, grappling with the concept of an unidentified anomaly deep within the Earth's crust. "An anomaly... What could that possibly entail?" she questioned aloud, her mind racing with possibilities and uncertainties.

Patterson maintained a serious expression, her tone measured. "At this point, we cannot provide a definitive answer," she responded. "That's precisely why we have assembled a team of experts like yourself. We need to conduct a thorough investigation to unravel the nature and implications of this anomaly. However, please understand that there are certain details that I'm unable to disclose at this time."

Dr. Williams nodded, realizing the gravity of the situation and the need for confidentiality in such matters. The call to action and the mystery surrounding the anomaly only heightened her determination to contribute her expertise to the team and uncover the truth concealed within the depths of the Earth. "I'm ready to contribute in any way I can. What's our next course of action?"

Dr. Patterson smiled appreciatively at Dr. Williams's readiness to contribute. "Thank you for your willingness to assist. We will share more details and provide a comprehensive briefing to the entire team shortly," she assured.

Realizing that there may be individuals in the room unfamiliar with the sites in question, Dr. Patterson turned her attention to Dr. Williams. "Dr. Williams, could you kindly provide us with a concise overview of the Kola Superdeep Borehole and Project Mohole, we'll be discussing? It appears that several individuals here are not familiar with them," she requested.

Dr. Williams pondered the scope of the presentation. "To what extent would you like the overview? Are you looking for a high-level summary or a more detailed presentation?" she inquired, seeking clarity on the level of information needed to bring everyone up to speed.

"Just general background, including the purpose, location, successes, and current utilization, if any, of the two sites," Patterson replied. "So far there has been no activity at the Project Mohole dig site, but you might include some about that also."

Dr. Williams, a little confused, is left standing as Patterson walks towards the head table and approaches the podium. She tapped on the microphone getting everyone's attention.

"Hello, my name is Judith Patterson. I am deputy director of the National Security Agency. I apologize for disrupting your lives but as you are about to learn, we are faced with a global crisis. One so grave that the Russian government has reached out for our assistance." She nods at military personnel on the perimeter of the room who start handing out documents and pens.

"Before we can proceed, I need to ensure everyone's commitment to confidentiality. You will all be required to sign a Non-Disclosure Agreement (NDA) immediately. Please understand that signing the NDA is necessary to protect the sensitive and top-secret nature of the material. Once you've signed, we can proceed with the discussion." No one objected and everyone turned in their NDA.

"Again, thank you for being here today. Each of you has been selected based on your expertise in various scientific disciplines. I must inform you that two significant events have unfolded in the past 48 hours, and if not addressed promptly, they pose grave consequences for our world. Time is of the essence, and we need to act swiftly to tackle these challenges." Small talk breaks out among the scientists. Patterson raises her hand.

"Please, please. We need to continue." Silence fills the room. She turns on her computer and on a giant screen behind her, Dr. Williams immediately recognizes the Kola Superdeep Borehole and the site of Project Mohole. "For those of you not familiar with these two locations, I would like to introduce Dr. Williams, professor of geology at Duke University, who is very familiar with these two sites and can give us an overview. Dr. Williams, if you please."

Dr. Williams, blushing, rises and walks up to the podium. "Good evening, everyone. As the deputy director mentioned, my name is Dr. Emily Williams. I am a professor of geology at Duke University. While I wasn't prepared to make a presentation tonight, Ms. Patterson has asked me to give you an overview of these two significant sites." Dr. Williams gestures towards the screen behind her, where a slide with two images are displayed side-by-side.

"The picture on the right shows the remains of the Kola Superdeep Borehole. It is located in the city of Murmansk, in the Arctic region of Russia. It was initiated during the Cold War by the Soviets and served as competition with the United States to determine which country could delve the deepest into the Earth's crust." The audience leans forward, captivated by the intriguing introduction.

"The borehole was an ambitious project, aiming to reach unprecedented depths. However, due to various challenges, it was eventually halted. Nonetheless, it left behind a testament to human determination and scientific exploration." The nervousness she initially felt had subsided. She takes a sip of water and continues.

"The Kola dig occurred near the Russian border with Norway, on the Kola Peninsula. There were several boreholes at the Kola site. Prior to closing the site in 1989, it reached a depth of 12,262 meters or almost 8 miles. It is still the deepest human-made hole on Earth. The drilling terminated in 1995 due to a lack of funds since the strife of the fall of the Soviet Union. The borehole was secured with a heavy-duty metal cap encased in concrete."

"As for Project Mohole, the project suffered from political and scientific opposition, mismanagement, and cost overruns. The U.S. House of Representatives defunded it in 1966. It succeeded in drilling to a depth of only 183 meters or 601 feet below the sea floor.

"While such a project was not feasible on land, drilling in the open ocean was more feasible, because the mantle lies much closer to the sea floor. Even though Project Mohole was not successful, the idea led to projects such as NSF's Deep Sea Drilling Project, and attempts to drill to extraordinary depths have continued." Dr. Williams adjusts her posture, projecting confidence as she continues.

Judith Patterson interrupts Dr. Williams. "Dr. Williams. I think that is adequate background information about the two sites, but will you please discuss what was learned from the Kola dig?" Dr. Williams is a little puzzled but as she provides the information starts realizing the relevance.

"Sure. One of the more fascinating findings to emerge is that no transition from granite to basalt was found at the depth of about seven kilometers, where the velocity of seismic waves has a discontinuity. Instead, the change in the seismic wave velocity was caused by a metamorphic transition in the granite rock. In addition, the rock at that depth had been thoroughly fractured and was saturated with water, which was surprising. This water, unlike surface water, must have come from deep-crust minerals and had been unable to reach the surface because of a layer of impermeable rock." There is more small talk in the audience.

"Even more amazing was the microscopic plankton fossils were found six kilometers below the surface. Another unexpected discovery was a large quantity of hydrogen gas. The drilling mud that flowed out of the hole was described as "boiling" with hydrogen." More talking breaks out between scientists. Dr. Williams turns towards Patterson who stands indicating she was pleased with her presentation. She takes over the podium and the crowd quiets down. Dr. Stevenson raises his hand before she begins. She recognizes him and he stands and addresses her.

"Although I find this very interesting, I fail to see how my background and expertise can help. I mean, what does the scientific study of arachnids have to do with two abandoned dig sites?"

"That's a very good question Dr. Stevenson. I'm sure your colleagues are also questioning how their field of expertise has anything to do with the Kola Superdeep Borehole." Patterson looks at a person sitting at the table and nods at him. As he approaches the podium Patterson makes an introduction. Dr. Williams noticed that Patterson only referred to the Kola site, not Project Mohole.

"Ladies and gentlemen, I would like to introduce Dr. Nikolai Ivanov from the Moscow University. Dr. Ivanov is an expert in Structural Geology. His research involving the study of deformation, fracturing, and folding of the earth's crust, including the processes underlying how mountains and volcanoes are formed are on the cutting edge of science and I'm sure many of you have read his research."

Dr. Ivanov, early seventies, bald, short, with a strong Russian accent, walks to the podium as Patterson takes a seat. He advances a slide showing the Kola dig site in shambles. Dr. Williams whispers to Dr. Carter. "I read his latest paper. It was brilliant."

"I met him once maybe ten years ago. He has really aged," Dr. Carter replied.

"Thank you, Director Patterson, for that kind introduction. Ladies and gentlemen, esteemed colleagues, today I stand before you with not only groundbreaking scientific revelations but also a dire warning that threatens the very fabric of our existence." The crowd's curiosity shifts to concern, their attention now fully captivated.

"Recently, a catastrophic event has unfolded in an area of the Kola dig site." As Dr. Williams explained the dig site was once covered by a protective cap, sealing its secrets deep beneath the Earth's surface. But I regret to inform you that the cap has erupted, breaching the containment and the borehole has enlarged." Gasps and murmurs ripple through the crowd as the scientists exchange worried glances.

"What has emerged from this catastrophic breach is beyond comprehension." Tension filled the room, the scientists realizing the gravity of the situation.

"A few days ago, two of our inspectors whose job it is to inspect the Kola site and examine that the cap is still in place, did not return from their trip. After being unsuccessful in reaching them on their cell phones, a second team of inspectors were sent to the site. When they arrived, they found this."

Dr. Ivanov advances a slide showing a demolished van covered with spider webs. Dr. Stevenson leans forward focused on the slide. A second slide is shown. "This is a close up of the borehole and as you can see, the cap was completely blown off and the size of the hole is now over 10' in circumference. You can also notice the hole is covered with cobwebs." Dr. Stevenson raises his hand, but again, Patterson motions for him to wait for Q&A later. A slide is advanced.

A close-up of the van shows claw like indentations which ripped through the sheet metal. "I caution you before I advance the next slides showing the two inspectors." Slides showing only the skeletal remains of two bodies partially wrapped in webbing filled the screen. Dr. Williams and Carter turn away.

"Due to the snowfall, no tracks were found. It is assumed that something emerged from the borehole and after killing our two inspectors, retreated. That, Dr. Stevenson, is why you are here. Our second team of inspectors took these slides but since dusk was approaching, they left and returned to the office." He hesitated as if he had more to share but kept the information to himself. He turns to Patterson who starts to stand.

Dr. Ivanov added a final comment. "We are hoping that this group, after visiting the Kola site, can help my country determine what is occurring. Thank you." As Dr. Ivanov takes his seat, Patterson, once again, goes to the podium.

"Ladies and gentlemen, there you have it. The President has offered our assistance to the Russian government in their investigation of the Kola Superdeep borehole. You have a 10 to 11 hour flight ahead of you. You will be leaving in one hour so if you need to make any phone calls or make arrangements, do so now."

Dr. Williams gazes at Dr. Carter and shakes her head. "So much for questions and answers. Fascinating, isn't it? I need to give my neighbor a call and check up on my daughter. Hopefully, they'll provide us with something to stay warm."

"Why is that necessary? Where exactly is the Kola site?" inquires Dr. Carter.

"Like I said, it's situated near the Russian border with Norway. Anticipate temperatures ranging from a high of 20°C to a low of 10°C. We can only expect about 6 hours of daylight at best."

Dr. Williams, Dr. Carter, and Dr. Ivanov, along with the other scientists, accompanied the group from the hangar to the tarmac, where they spotted the large C-5M Super Galaxy plane. As they boarded the aircraft, they noticed the presence of the three military officers from the briefing, accompanied by twenty heavily armed uniformed Army soldiers and a general.

An announcement came over the PA system from the unseen pilot. "Ladies and gentlemen, we have a lengthy flight ahead of us. The NSA has provided food and non-alcoholic beverages for you towards the rear of the plane. Please be mindful of the military vehicles in that area. Once we reach cruising altitude, feel free to help yourselves. The Arctic air can sometimes make for a bumpy ride, but I'll do my best to find smoother air. Thank you."

Once the plane reached its cruising altitude, a green light illuminated, indicating that the passengers were now free to access the food. Most of the scientists took advantage of this, while the soldiers refrained from doing so. With their food in hand, the scientists made their way back to their seats. General Terrence Hargrove then stood up.

In an authoritative voice, he addressed the group of scientists. "Ladies and gentlemen, I am General Hargrove. I have been entrusted with the leadership of this expedition. As our pilot mentioned, we have an estimated 11- hour flight ahead of us to Murmansk, Russia. Upon our arrival, the Russian government has graciously arranged rooms for each of you. Depending on our arrival time, I will determine how long we can rest before proceeding to the site. We only have sunlight from 10 am to 4 pm, so it is crucial that we arrive and establish our camp, before nightfall."

Dr. Stevenson decided to interject with a question. "General, what is the military's perspective on this incident?"

General Hargrove pauses before he responds. "With all due respect to Dr. Ivanov, I have dedicated my life to defending our nation against tangible threats. Directing our resources and military capabilities to fly halfway around the world to combat oversized arachnids, in my opinion, is a misuse of those resources."

A defiant Dr. Ivanov replies. "General Hargrove, I understand your concerns. These creatures may seem fantastical, but the evidence we have gathered so far indicates that they pose a serious threat. They possess extraordinary abilities and demonstrate advanced social organization. If left unchecked, they could unleash unimaginable chaos and devastation," replied Dr. Ivanov. General Hargrove's stern expression softened slightly as he contemplated Dr. Ivanov's words.

"Dr. Ivanov, I respect your expertise, but forgive me for needing more concrete evidence before I can fully commit our military forces to this endeavor. My primary mission is to protect you scientists. But, if the situation calls for the use of force, we are prepared". Dr. Ivanov nods, understanding the need for tangible proof.

"General Hargrove, I appreciate your cautious approach. I want to assure you that we are actively collecting additional evidence and data to strengthen our claims. Confronting this threat requires the collaboration and support of various disciplines, including military expertise. You have witnessed the footage. We firmly believe that these creatures are indeed real," Dr. Ivanov expressed, addressing both the scientists and General Hargrove. He gravely turns and looks at the assemble group.

"General, ladies and gentlemen, I have been instructed by the NSA to share the following information and show you the evidence, but only after we became airborne to prevent any potential panic if this were to reach the public." Suspense fills the air as everyone exchanges glances. Dr. Ivanov reaches into his backpack and retrieves a large laptop, switching it on.

"As I mentioned during our earlier briefing, after the first team of inspectors failed to return from their mission, we dispatched a second team. However, what I was specifically instructed to withhold from you is the fact that only a few members of the second team survived their inspection." The cabin of the plane falls into a profound silence, interrupted only by the powerful roar of the engines. "I apologize for the gravity of this information. I request that all of you gather around me to view the screen."

As General Hargrove and the other scientists positioned themselves around Dr. Ivanov, the soldiers remained seated, their attention focused on the unfolding scene. Dr. Ivanov proceeds to play a video footage on the laptop screen.

"What has transpired following this catastrophic breach is utterly incomprehensible. We are facing creatures that resemble spiders, but on an unimaginable scale. They have seized control of the region, posing a significant threat not only to the scientific community but to humanity as a whole," Dr. Ivanov explains, his voice filled with concern and urgency.

General Hargrove's skepticism momentarily lingers in the tense atmosphere as Dr. Ivanov initiates the video file. The jerky footage captures the harrowing scene as screams echo in the background. Several spider-like creatures emerge from the borehole, their elongated limbs skittering across the snowy landscape. Towering at least 6 feet tall, their bodies become a grotesque fusion of insects and arachnids—a horrifying combination of chitinous armor and spindly legs.

Every occupant of the plane becomes captivated by the video, their attention fully absorbed by the disturbing images. Eventually, breaking the silence, Dr. Ivanov speaks. "These spider-like creatures possess astonishing intelligence, formidable strength, and an insatiable hunger for dominance. Our initial observations suggest that they have already begun exhibiting coordinated behavior, organizing themselves into highly complex societies that surpass anything we have witnessed in the animal kingdom."

"As you witnessed, these adult creatures stand at approximately 6 feet tall, with heads that resemble a fusion of a spider and a mantis," Dr. Ivanov continues, his tone filled with a mix of awe and dread. "Their exoskeletons emit a sickly green sheen, a haunting sight to behold.

In this particular video, we can see a female specimen carrying her young on her back, much like a wolf spider. It's a chilling display of their reproductive behavior." Dr. Ivanov glances at Dr. Stevenson, who nods in agreement, affirming the accuracy of his statement.

"These creatures possess multiple sets of beady, luminescent eyes that pierce through the darkness," Dr. Ivanov adds, emphasizing their eerie features. "Their jagged mandibles click and snap, revealing droplets of acidic venom dripping from their razor-sharp fangs." A wave of unease courses through the cabin as the scientists and passengers grapple with the magnitude of the situation unfolding before them.

Dr. Ivanov's urgency fills his plea as he continues, "These spider-like creatures possess the ability to expel jets of corrosive acid from specialized glands within their twisted mouths. It is imperative that each and every one of us sets aside our individual pursuits and joins forces. We must unite our expertise, resources, and collective intellect to confront this unparalleled threat."

A profound silence descends upon the plane as the scientists process the information presented . Dr. Ivanov's words hang in the air, resonating with the weight of the challenge they now face. "General Hargrove, we must formulate a comprehensive strategy to contain, study, and ultimately eradicate these spider-like creatures. Our very existence hinges upon swift and resolute action," he concludes, closing his laptop and delving into deep contemplation.

The cabin remains enveloped in silence, each individual grappling with the enormity of the task at hand and contemplating the shared responsibility that now rests upon their shoulders.

General Hargrove, still grappling with the shocking revelations, remains speechless as the weight of the situation sinks in. It is Dr. Carter who breaks the silence, posing a pertinent question to Dr. Ivanov.

"Dr. Ivanov, were there any volcanic activities or earthquakes leading up to the eruption of the Kola cap?" Dr. Carter inquires, seeking to understand any potential geological factors involved.

"Yes," Dr. Ivanov responds with a solemn nod. "We had been monitoring small shockwaves both before, during, and after the eruption of the cap on the borehole. These seismic activities have persisted following the incident."

His response indicates that there were indeed geological disturbances preceding the emergence of the spider-like creatures, suggesting a possible correlation between the two events. The scientists exchange concerned glances as they consider the implications of this information.

Dr. Carter follows up with another question, seeking to understand the findings from the dig site. "As you mentioned, what have your scientists discovered at the dig site?" Dr. Carter inquires, eager to gather more information.

Dr. Ivanov's expression turns somber as he responds, "When our second team arrived at the site, they discovered the inspection van that had been used by our previous team. Tragically, they found the skeletal remains of our colleagues entangled within webs that enveloped their bodies. At dusk, these very creatures emerged from the borehole and launched a vicious attack."

His words convey the grim reality of the situation, underscoring the danger that awaits anyone who ventures into the vicinity of these formidable spider-like creatures. The weight of the discoveries weighs heavily on the minds of those present, intensifying the need for a swift and decisive response to this escalating threat.

Dr. Stevenson, having absorbed the information and observations, finally speaks up, drawing on his expertise as an Arachnologist. "Dr. Ivanov, as an Arachnologist, I am simply astounded by what I have witnessed. Your description of these creatures possessing traits of both spiders and mantises is accurate.

There is a family of spiders called Scytodidae, commonly known as spitting spiders, which includes 239 species found worldwide. Some of these spiders can shoot a deadly liquid silk at astonishing speeds of nearly 30 meters per second. They tend to be nocturnal, seeking shelter in dark crevices, closets, and under rocks during the day. Fortunately, they pose no threat to humans and are typically the size of ordinary garden spiders."

Dr. Ivanov acknowledges Dr. Stevenson's input, affirming, "Dr. Stevenson, you have indeed touched upon something that aligns with our initial observations at the site. These creatures appear to exhibit heightened activity during the night and respond with fear and aggression when exposed to sunlight."

This realization adds a significant layer to the understanding of the creatures' behavior and provides a potential avenue for strategic intervention. The scientists contemplate this newfound knowledge, recognizing that the creatures' nocturnal nature could be an advantage in planning their approach to contain and confront the threat they pose.

Dr. Williams raises an important point regarding the size of the borehole at Kola, drawing from her experience at both the Project Mohole and Kola dig sites. She seeks clarification from Dr. Ivanov. "Dr. Ivanov, based on my recollection, the actual borehole at Kola was only 9 inches in diameter. Can you please inform us of the current size of the hole?"

Dr. Ivanov responds, "A few days ago, the hole had expanded to at least 10 feet in circumference. However, it is difficult to provide an exact measurement now, as each time one of these creatures emerges, the friction of their passage causes the hole to increase in size. Since the attack on our previous team, we have been unable to approach the hole and gather precise measurements."

Dr. Williams acknowledges his response, then proceeds with a follow-up question. "Understood. In light of the depth of over 40,000 feet, do your scientists genuinely believe that these creatures could survive at such extreme depths?"

Dr. Ivanov sighs, conveying the uncertainty surrounding this aspect. "I wish I could provide a definitive answer, Doctor. Among our scientific team, there are differing opinions. Some believe that over the years of the borehole's shutdown, these creatures may have tunneled from a lower level and, upon reaching the Kola borehole, simply utilized it as a pathway to reach the surface." The explanation suggests a possibility that the creatures found their way to the surface through an alternative underground network, raising further questions about their origins and adaptability."

General Hargrove directs his question to Dr. Ivanov, inquiring about the use of weaponry by the second team during their encounter with the creatures.

"No, General," Dr. Ivanov responds. "The second team was ill-prepared for what they encountered. They were caught off guard and found themselves defenseless. Only a few managed to escape with their lives."

General Hargrove falls silent, deep in thought, before addressing the group of scientists once again. "Well, ladies and gentlemen, we still have several hours before reaching our destination. I suggest that we utilize this time to strategize how we can either confront or contain these creatures," he advises, his tone reflecting the urgency of the situation. With that, he walks towards the rear of the plane, engaging in private conversations with his fellow military personnel while also taking a moment for sustenance and refreshments.

The scientists are left to contemplate the weight of the task before them, realizing the need to develop a plan that can effectively address the threat posed by the spider-like creatures.

Dr. Carter approaches Dr. Ivanov, seeking information regarding seismic activity before, during, and after the emergence of the creatures. Dr. Ivanov promptly retrieves the relevant data from his computer files, displaying it on the screen. As Dr. Carter examines the information, her eyes widen in a mixture of disbelief and horror, realizing the significance of the findings.

"If we observe these spikes on the graphs," Dr. Carter explains, pointing at the screen, "it aligns with what you mentioned. This spike corresponds to the date and time when your first inspection team arrived at the site. The second spike likely represents the moment when the cap blew off, marking the emergence of the spiders. However, what is truly intriguing is that these smaller spikes appear to be almost constant."

The other scientists watch intently as Dr. Carter connects the dots, recognizing the potential correlation between the seismic activity and the emergence of the creatures. The implications of this discovery reverberate through the cabin, heightening the urgency to understand the underlying causes and dynamics at play.

Dr. Stevenson poses a question, seeking clarification on the significance of the constant activity in the borehole. "It suggests that the activity within the borehole is ongoing," Dr. Carter responds, her voice filled with a mix of concern and intrigue. General Hargrove briefly observes the scientists' discussion before walking away, his mind grappling with the implications of the continuing activity within the borehole. Dr. Williams, seizing the opportunity, asks Dr. Ivanov about the data regarding samples taken from the dig site before its closure.

"Yes, give me a moment," Dr. Ivanov responds, quickly accessing the desired information on his computer. A new graph appears on the screen, capturing the attention of Dr. Williams and Dr. Carter.

Dr. Williams leans forward, her voice filled with surprise, "Look at this. This mineral composition is highly unusual. And these samples contain dormant life forms. It's extraordinary. These findings suggest the presence of a long-lost ecosystem buried beneath the Earth's crust."

Dr. Carter, intrigued by the revelations, requests Dr. Ivanov to bring up seismic data from the Project Mohole site for comparison. "I don't have that data. The Americans kept their information highly secretive, even after all these years. There was competition between the two sites during their operational periods," Dr. Ivanov explains.

Dr. Carter ponders the information, her gaze shifting between Dr. Williams and the screen. After a brief pause, she responds, "I'm thinking that there is a possibility that something similar might be occurring at the Project Mohole site, although perhaps not to the same magnitude as Kola."

The scientists recognize the potential parallel between the two sites, raising further concerns about the extent and nature of the underground ecosystems and the potential threat they pose.

After a restful eight hours of sleep in Murmansk, the group arrives at the Kola site. They find that the soldiers have already set up a temporary camp near the borehole, positioned away from the damaged inspection van. The scientists waste no time and begin their examination of the remnants left behind by the previous Russian inspection teams.

Dr. Stevenson, displaying meticulous attention to detail, carefully collects tissue samples from one of the corpses. With great care, he extracts fragments of the intricate webbing that surrounds the body. Dr. Williams and Dr. Carter observe with a mix of fascination and curiosity as they witness the precision and expertise of their colleague.

The examination of the remains and the intricate webbing presents the scientists with a wealth of data and new avenues for investigation. They feel a sense of urgency as they delve deeper into the mysteries surrounding the creatures and the implications they hold for the world.

Dr. Williams, feeling a hint of a blush, engages Dr. Stevenson in conversation, curious to hear his thoughts on the arachnid species they are dealing with. "Dr. Stevenson, what are your thoughts on this? Have you ever encountered an arachnid of this magnitude capable of spewing acid?" she asks, finding him quite handsome.

"Please, call me Paul," he replies with a warm smile.

"Only if you call me Emily," she responds, feeling a slight blush creeping onto her cheeks. "So, what is your take on all of this?"

Paul takes a moment to gather his thoughts before answering, "The arachnid species that exhibits a similar method of killing is the Scytodidae. They are known for capturing their prey by spitting a fluid that rapidly congeals upon contact, transforming into a venomous and adhesive mass. This fluid is a combination of venom and spider silk in a liquid state, originating from venom glands within their chelicerae."

Emily, feeling a little rusty on her biology knowledge, asks, "Sorry, it's been a long time since I took a biology class. What exactly are chelicerae?"

Paul kindly explains, "No problem. Chelicerae are the pair of appendages located in front of the mouth in arachnids and some other arthropods. They are usually modified as pincer-like claws. These creatures we're dealing with also share another characteristic. After capturing their prey, they typically bite it with venomous effect and then wrap it in the typical spider fashion, using silk produced from their spinnerets. It's just like what we see here with this victim."

Emily listens intently, appreciating Paul's expertise and the insights he brings to the discussion. The conversation deepens their connection and strengthens their collaboration as they grapple with the extraordinary nature of the creatures they are studying.

General Hargrove, observing the dusk descending upon the Kola site, becomes aware of the approaching evening. As he contemplates the situation, a soldier approaches and offers a salute. "General, we completed a thorough reconnaissance of the surrounding area," the soldier reports. "Due to the snow cover, we couldn't find any tracks. However, we did come across peculiar cave-like openings on certain parts of the hillsides. It's unclear what they signify, but they are certainly unusual."

Acknowledging the soldier's report, General Hargrove responds, "Thank you, Private. Make sure to get yourself some coffee and grab something to eat. You've done well." Recognizing the importance of the soldier's findings, General Hargrove understands that further investigation is necessary to determine the significance of these mysterious cave-like openings. The soldiers, too, deserve a moment to refresh and refuel after their diligent work.

As dusk envelops the surroundings, the scientists and General Hargrove gather inside the main tent, creating a space for discussion and sharing their findings. Dr. Ivanov, driven by curiosity, directs his question to Dr. Stevenson, acknowledging his expertise in arachnids.

"Dr. Stevenson, with your extensive knowledge on arachnids, have you developed any speculations or hypotheses regarding these creatures?"

Dr. Stevenson clears his throat, preparing to share his thoughts. "Based on my preliminary analysis," he begins, "these creatures do exhibit certain characteristics reminiscent of spitting spiders. Their predatory behavior aligns with that of those spiders. However, in terms of their immense size and the acidic substance they spew, as seen on your laptop, there is nothing on Earth that even comes close to comparison."

Pausing for a moment to let the gravity of his words sink in, Dr. Stevenson continues, "I conducted an analysis of the acid I extracted from one of the victims. The chemical breakdown shows similarities, but it is far more toxic than the venom of the Sidney Funnel Web spider found in Australia. Typically, male funnel-web spiders are solitary, but females have been known to live in colonies of over 100 spiders or more."

The revelation of the creatures' unprecedented size, their deadly acid, and the possibility of communal behavior among the females leaves the group in awe, further emphasizing the extraordinary nature of the situation they face.

General Hargrove, having overheard the conversation, responds with skepticism, challenging the notion that these creatures originated from the center of the Earth. "So, Doctor," he scoffs, "you agree with your colleagues' belief that these creatures originated from the center of the Earth?"

Dr. Stevenson, maintaining his composure, addresses the general's skepticism. "Well, General Hargrove, while I understand the skepticism surrounding such a hypothesis, I must admit that the evidence we've encountered thus far suggests a possibility that cannot be easily dismissed. The extraordinary size and unique attributes of these creatures do raise intriguing questions about their origin. It's imperative that we remain open-minded as we continue our investigation and gather more data."

The general then turns his attention to Drs. Carter and Williams, seeking their agreement with Dr. Stevenson's assessment. "And what about you, Dr. Carter and Dr. Williams? Do you both concur with Dr. Stevenson's assessment?" General Hargrove inquires.

Dr. Williams takes the opportunity to present her perspective, slightly diverging from Dr. Stevenson's viewpoint. "General, I have a slightly different perspective than Paul, I mean Dr. Stevenson," she replies. "I believe these creatures originated from beneath the Earth's crust rather than the center. The discovery of dormant life forms prior to the sealing of the Kola borehole indicates the presence of an ecosystem within the layers of rock formations. It is plausible that recent seismic activity disturbed their habitat, causing them to awaken and utilize the borehole as a convenient passage to the surface."

Dr. Carter joins in, supporting Dr. Williams' perspective. "I agree with Dr. Williams," she asserts. "These spider-like creatures emerged from the depths of the Earth, either due to seismic activity or a disruption caused by the drilling operation. For centuries, they remained hidden and undisturbed in their subterranean realm. The recent earth tremors may have disturbed their environment, prompting them to explore the surface of the Earth."

The differing viewpoints among the scientists highlight the complexity of the situation and the need for further investigation to uncover the truth about the creatures' origins and motivations.

Dr. Stevenson, firm in his beliefs, reiterates his perspective. "These creatures must have undergone remarkable adaptations to survive in the deepest recesses of the Earth, far removed from human presence. The constant vibrations caused by the relentless exploration efforts in this region likely disrupted the delicate balance of their underground habitat."

His words carry conviction, emphasizing the importance of understanding the profound impact human activities can have on the delicate ecosystems that exist beneath the Earth's surface. The scientists and General Hargrove contemplate the implications of these disruptions and the subsequent emergence of the spider-like creatures, recognizing the need for caution and a comprehensive approach in dealing with the situation at hand.

General Hargrove, still harboring skepticism, raises an important question regarding the absence of the creatures at the Project Mohole site. "But why haven't they emerged from the ground at the Project Mohole site? They conducted drilling there as well, didn't they?" he queries.

Dr. Williams, ready with an answer, responds, "General, Project Mohole was ultimately unsuccessful in reaching significant depths. It only managed to penetrate 3,600 meters, with most of that depth consisting of ocean water before reaching the sea floor. As a result, the drilling efforts produced significantly less vibration compared to the ongoing drilling here at Kola. It's possible that the creatures were undisturbed due to the limited impact on their underground habitat."

General Hargrove absorbs this explanation, beginning to grasp the complexities of the situation they face. Drawing a parallel to science fiction films, he expresses his concern and desire to find a way to contain and, if necessary, eliminate the creatures. All of this sounds like something out of a science fiction movie," he muses. "Like those Godzilla films where nefarious individuals introduce radiation into the environment, and then Mother Nature retaliates with a monstrous creature. What I want to know is how we can contain these creatures and, if necessary, how to eliminate them?"

The gravity of the situation weighs upon the group as they contemplate the potential consequences of these creatures' existence. The challenge ahead is not only understanding their origin but also devising a plan to ensure the safety of humanity and the delicate balance of the ecosystem.

The group's intense discussion is abruptly shattered by the jarring sound of M4 carbine fire, followed by piercing screams and a whirlwind of chaos. The air is thick with urgency and panic as the chilling clicking sound of mandibles fills the air. General Hargrove, instantly alert, swiftly exits the tent, urgently instructing the scientists to remain inside and stay safe.

Dr. Williams and Dr. Stevenson exchange concerned glances, their hearts racing with a mix of curiosity and fear. Unable to resist their innate curiosity, they cautiously approach a small opening in the tent's flap, their eyes peering through the gap. What they witness is a scene straight from their worst nightmares.

Outside, a horrifying sight unfolds before them. Several soldiers are engaged in a desperate battle against the enormous spiders. The soldiers unleash a relentless barrage of rifle and small arms fire, their weapons aiming at the monstrous creatures. But their efforts prove futile and disheartening. The bullets ricochet off the spiders' thick exoskeletons, failing to slow them down even for a moment.

Dr. Williams and Dr. Stevenson exchange a mix of shock and realization. The sheer resilience and ferocity of the creatures become starkly apparent in that moment. The scientists understand the immense challenge they face and the urgent need to find a way to neutralize these seemingly invulnerable foes.

Dr. Stevenson's words hang in the air, emphasizing the urgent need for a more powerful solution against the resilient creatures. Dr. Williams and Dr. Stevenson watch in horrified disbelief as the spiders deftly maneuver, using their agile bodies and deadly mandibles to overpower the soldiers one by one. The symphony of screams and the relentless clicking of mandibles create a chilling atmosphere of terror.

A surge of determination washes over them as they witness the soldiers' resourcefulness. The soldiers, recognizing the futility of conventional weapons, resort to the use of hand grenades. Explosions punctuate the chaos as the grenades prove devastatingly effective against the formidable creatures. The sight of the spiders being torn apart by the force of the explosions fills the scientists with both relief and a sense of grim satisfaction.

Dr. Stevenson tightly grips Dr. Williams' arm, their faces etched with fear and awe. They exchange glances, their eyes reflecting the horrors they have witnessed. The campsite resonates with the cacophony of explosions, shattering the arachnids into grotesque fragments. The remaining soldiers swiftly follow suit, joining the fight with a renewed determination to eliminate the monstrous creatures that threaten their lives.

In the face of this newfound knowledge about the spiders' vulnerability to explosive force, the scientists and soldiers must now devise a strategy to effectively harness the power of explosives and ensure the safety of all those involved.

Amidst the aftermath of the intense battle, some of the surviving creatures frantically scurry toward the borehole, seeking refuge in the depths from which they emerged. Others, however, find shelter within the enigmatic cave-like structures concealed beneath the snowy landscape. Motionless soldiers lie partially trapped in sticky webbing, their bodies bearing the agonizing wounds inflicted by the creatures' corrosive acid.

Reacting swiftly, the scientists rush to provide much-needed first aid to the wounded soldiers, doing their best to alleviate their pain and stabilize their conditions. General Hargrove, his voice cutting through the chaos, shouts commands to a sergeant, determined to fortify their defenses.

"Sergeant, I want several men stationed at each entrance on the hillside and positioned over the borehole," the General orders. "If those bastards attempt to emerge from those openings, I want them blasted back to hell."

Simultaneously, General Hargrove gestures for a communication officer to approach him, understanding the urgency of the situation. "You," he addresses the officer, "report in immediately. Inform our command that we have come under attack and have sustained several casualties. Request immediate reinforcements, including flamethrowers, additional hand grenades, and high-end explosives. We need all the firepower we can get to combat this threat."

The General's resolute demeanor reflects the gravity of the situation and his commitment to protecting his team and eradicating the menacing creatures. With the reinforcements and increased firepower, they hope to reclaim control over the situation and prevent any further loss of life.

A corporal approaches General Hargrove, offering a crisp salute. "General," he begins, "we have only two operational vehicles, both Humvees. However, we can salvage our remaining supplies. Our ammunition and grenade stocks are low, but fortunately, the creatures did not damage our fuel reserves."

Acknowledging the corporal's report, General Hargrove nods his appreciation. "Thank you, corporal," he responds. "Take up a position near the borehole. Ensure the remaining vehicles are ready for deployment and gather any salvageable supplies. We need to make the most of what we have."

The corporal acknowledges the order with a salute before swiftly carrying out the General's instructions. As he moves into action, preparations are underway to fortify the defense positions near the borehole, while the remaining operational Humvees are readied for potential future operations. The urgency to secure the area and replenish their dwindling resources is palpable, highlighting the importance of resourcefulness and efficient utilization of their limited assets in their ongoing battle against the menacing creatures.

General Hargrove's face reflects a mixture of concern and determination as he steps back into the tent, where the scientists and remaining soldiers await his next words. With a grave tone, he addresses the group, acknowledging his previous underestimation of the creatures they face.

"Ladies and gentlemen," he begins, his voice laced with humility, "I must humbly admit that I underestimated the cunning and resilience of these creatures. It's clear that our small arms fire is ineffective against their formidable exoskeletons. Furthermore, our limited supply of grenades poses a significant cause for concern."

The weight of the situation hangs heavy in the air, with the soldiers and scientists exchanging solemn glances. General Hargrove's admission of their current limitations serves as a reminder of the urgent need for alternative strategies and increased firepower.

"We cannot rely solely on our existing weaponry," the General continues, his voice firm. "We must think creatively and utilize any available resources to gain the upper hand. Our survival and the safety of all those involved depend on it." His words resonate throughout the tent, emphasizing the need for a shift in approach and a relentless pursuit of solutions. The scientists and soldiers understand the gravity they face, recognizing that they must adapt and overcome the challenges posed by these extraordinary creatures if they are to have any chance of success.

Dr. Emily Williams, driven by urgency and determination, speaks up, seeking a plan of action from General Hargrove. The General prepares to outline their next steps.

"We need to adapt and strategize," General Hargrove begins, his voice firm. "We cannot rely solely on the firepower we currently possess. We must maximize the utilization of our available resources while we await reinforcements." Pausing for a moment to gather his thoughts, the General continues, addressing the soldiers directly.

"First and foremost, we must establish strong defensive positions. Post additional guards at each entrance on the hillside and maintain constant vigilance over the borehole. We must repel any further attempts by these creatures to breach our defenses."

His gaze then shifts to the scientists, emphasizing the need for precision and strategic thinking. "As for the scientists, you must focus on targeting the creatures' weak spots and areas where we can inflict the most damage. Our remaining grenades must be utilized wisely—each throw counts."

Acknowledging the ongoing efforts to secure reinforcements, General Hargrove informs the group, "Our communication officer has already requested immediate reinforcements, including flamethrowers and additional high-end explosives. We must hold the line until they arrive. That will be in 72-hours."

Dr. Ivanov adds to the grim news by presenting a radar program on his laptop, displaying the massive Arctic front closing in on the Kola region. The imminent storm poses an additional challenge to their already precarious situation, increasing the urgency to fortify their defenses and endure until the reinforcements can join their fight.

With the plan outlined and the storm closing in, the group understands the critical nature of their mission. They must remain resolute and resourceful in the face of adversity, holding the line against the relentless onslaught of the creatures until help arrives. The countdown begins, and their battle for survival intensifies in the face of the impending storm and the overwhelming threat that lurks beneath the surface.

Emily, engrossed in her thoughts, breaks the silence with a determined tone. Her words carry the weight of necessity as she presents her perspective to the group. "In addition to our current plan, we must seek alternative methods," her voice filled with resolve. "We need to explore any potential vulnerabilities in these creatures, such as their sensitivity to certain stimuli or weaknesses we can exploit. Dr. Stevenson, I believe this falls under your expertise."

She pauses, allowing her words to sink in before continuing. "Furthermore, we must embrace innovation and be open to unconventional solutions. We are dealing with a formidable enemy, but we have one another. Together, we can overcome these challenges." The group, now united in their renewed sense of determination, nods in agreement. They understand the need to think outside the box.

Dr. Williams, Dr. Stevenson, General Hargrove, and the selected soldiers gather around the rough drawing spread out on the table, their expressions reflecting determination and resolve. Dr. Williams takes the lead, pointing to the cave-like structures depicted in the drawing.

"These cave-like structures in the hillside might hold some crucial answers," she explains, her voice filled with conviction. "If we can safely explore one of them, we could gain valuable insights into the creatures' behavior and vulnerabilities." She pauses momentarily, gauging the reactions of her fellow colleagues before continuing with her proposal.

"My idea, considering our ample fuel supply, is to pour a generous amount down the entrance of one of these caves and ignite it. Once the fire burns out, we can cautiously enter and investigate further. This approach could provide us with a chance to uncover vital information about the creatures' habitat and potential weaknesses. What do you all think?"

The room falls silent as the gravity of Dr. Williams' suggestion sinks in. General Hargrove and Dr. Stevenson exchange glances, considering the risks and potential benefits of the plan. After a moment of contemplation, General Hargrove speaks up.

"Dr. Williams, your proposal is indeed bold and carries risks, but it could also yield valuable insights. We must weigh the potential gains against the potential dangers involved. If executed properly, this approach could provide us with a unique opportunity to gather critical information."

Dr. Stevenson, a mix of caution and excitement in his eyes, adds his perspective. "It's a high-risk maneuver, but if we proceed with caution and ensure the safety of our team, it could be our best chance to understand these creatures on a deeper level."

With a collective understanding of the potential risks and rewards, the group reaches a consensus. They understand the need to push boundaries and explore uncharted territory in their quest for understanding and survival. The plan is set in motion, and preparations begin for the controlled ignition of the cave entrance.

Armed with determination and a shared commitment, they are prepared to face the unknown, taking calculated risks in their pursuit of knowledge and a means to combat the creatures. The fire that will illuminate the darkness of the cave also symbolizes their unwavering resolve and their refusal to succumb to fear. Together, they embark on this perilous endeavor, ready to confront whatever lies within and emerge with the insights that could turn the tide in their favor.

"Sounds like a plan," General Hargrove exclaims, his voice resolute. He swiftly turns to the soldiers gathered around and issues his orders with authority. "You heard what the doctor said. Start pouring gasoline and diesel down those entrances and torch them off." The soldiers, following the General's command, proceed to carry out the task. The sound of fuel being ignited fills the air, accompanied by the crackling flames and billowing smoke that engulf the cave entrances.

General Hargrove's attention then returns to the drawing, his gaze focused and determined. "Alright, we'll approach this cautiously," he declares, his voice calm but assertive. "The safety of our team is paramount. We will divide into two small groups, heavily armed and equipped with grenades. Remember, we are not there to engage in unnecessary combat. Our primary objective is reconnaissance."

His words hang in the air, emphasizing the importance of their mission. The team understands the significance of their task and the need for precision and vigilance. Each member gears up mentally and physically, preparing themselves for the challenges that lie ahead.

With their objectives defined, the soldiers form their groups, ensuring they are armed and ready for any potential encounter. Their steps are deliberate and cautious as they approach the burning entrances, mindful of the unknown dangers that await within. Their focus is on gathering valuable information, mapping out the territory, and assessing the creatures' behavior and vulnerabilities.

The small teams move forward, synchronized in their movements, their senses heightened, and their determination unwavering. They navigate the smoky environment, staying vigilant and communicating through subtle gestures and shared instincts. The flames continue to rage behind them, a constant reminder of their purpose and the risks they face.

A sergeant walks up and addresses the general. "Sir, I'd like to lead one of the teams. Those assholes killed Jimmy and Tito." General Hargrove studies the young sergeant.

"Good, Sergeant. Take Dr. Ivanov, Dr. Carter and two other scientists and pick four soldiers. I'll take Dr. Williams and Dr. Stevenson with me. Gear up, everyone. We leave in fifteen minutes."

He turns and addresses the others in the group. "The rest of you can team up with my men watching the other cave entrances and the borehole." The soldiers and scientists disperse, gathering their equipment and preparing for the dangerous mission ahead.

As they venture deeper into the scorched caves, their steps echoing in the darkness, they embody the spirit of reconnaissance, collecting vital intelligence that will shape their future actions. Every movement, every observation, is a piece of the puzzle that will aid them in their mission to overcome the relentless creatures and ensure the safety of all.

The sun was slowly creeping up giving a little sense of safety to the group, knowing that it would soon disappear as they entered the cave-like structures. Dr. Williams, Dr. Stevenson, and General Hargrove, and four soldiers make their way towards one of the structures. The other team lead by the sergeant, does the same. They move with calculated steps, their eyes scanning the surroundings for any signs of movement. As they approach the entrance of the structure, tension fills the air. A soldier motions for the team to halt. "Secure the area. Watch your backs. We don't know what we might encounter inside," he whispers.

The soldiers take their positions, their weapons at the ready. They enter the cave followed by General Hargrove, Dr. Williams and Dr. Stevenson, their scientific curiosity blending with a sense of trepidation. The lead soldiers turn on their flashlights and the scientists do the same. Dr. Williams carefully examines the structure, noting its unique characteristics. "The architecture of this structure is unlike anything I've seen before. It's as if the creatures have adapted these natural formations to suit their needs."

Dr. Stevenson nods, his eyes scanning the entrance for any signs of movement. With a deep breath, the group goes deeper into the cave-like structure, their senses heightened. The soldiers tightening their grip on their weapons. "I can't tell if this cave was dug from the inside or outside. It looks like it goes on for miles," Dr. Williams states as she continues to touch the walls of the cave.

The group ventures deeper into the darkened interior, their flashlight beams illuminating the mysterious environment. Strange webbing and remnants of the creatures' presence become increasingly apparent. They move silently, listening for any unusual sounds or movements. The air is heavy with anticipation and the unknown.

A low, haunting clicking echoes through the chamber, causing everyone to freeze in their tracks. Startled, the team turns to witness several spiders, their enormous forms crawling out from the depths of the tunnel system. Suddenly, the spiders strike, lunging at the soldiers with terrifying speed and ferocity. Gunfire erupts, lighting up the darkness as the battle ensues.

Soldiers and spiders clash in a desperate struggle. The soldiers fight valiantly, but the spiders' strength and agility pose a formidable challenge. Amidst the chaos, one soldier sustains a fatal wound, succumbing to the venomous bite of a spider. Dr. Stevenson reacts swiftly, pulling Dr. Williams away from immediate danger.

"We need to regroup! Fall back!" General Hargrove yells. The team retreats, keeping the remaining spiders at bay with well-aimed shots and explosives. The wounded soldier is carefully carried by his comrades, his sacrifice a grim reminder of the stakes they face. Take defensive positions! We can't let them gain ground. Hold the line!" The soldiers form a defensive perimeter, readying their weapons as Dr. Williams and Dr. Stevenson join their ranks, determination etched on their faces. General Hargrove orders a cautious retreat.

Dr. Ivanov, Dr. Carter, and the sergeant who volunteered to lead the group plus four soldiers cautiously enter the second cave. Their flashlights illuminating the dark, foreboding chamber. The air feels heavy with anticipation and tension. There is a slight ammonia smell. The sergeant turns and whispers to everyone, "Stay alert, everyone. We don't know what awaits us in here."

Dr. Carter nods. "Keep your eyes peeled for any signs of movement or unusual webbing. Stay close and watch each other's backs. How are you doing, Dr. Ivanov?"

"So far, so good but I think my hiking days are behind me." The team moves deeper into the cave, their footsteps echoing against the rocky walls. Suddenly, a low, menacing clicking sound reverberates through the chamber.

The sergeant whispers, "Do you hear that? Be ready for anything." The team proceeds further into the interconnected tunnels of the cave system. Shadows dance on the walls, creating an atmosphere of unease. Dr. Ivanov examines the intricate web patterns, noting their complexity. "Amazing, look at these webs. They're not like anything I've ever seen. Highly evolved and structurally intricate."

Dr. Carter's voice cuts through the tension, drawing attention to the scattered minerals and gems littering the cave floor. The team halts, their flashlights revealing the dazzling array of colors and sparkling formations. "These minerals and gems must have been carried by the creatures as they tunneled through the rock formations. It's a remarkable find." Dr. Carter and Dr. Ivanov step closer, their eyes widening with curiosity.

"The creatures inadvertently act as transporters, spreading minerals and gems through their movements. It could lead us to valuable insights about the geological composition of the region."

"I agree," Dr. Ivanov said as he continues to study the minerals. "If we can analyze the deposits, we might be able to trace their origin and potentially uncover hidden resources or unique geological features."

"This discovery could be a silver lining amidst the challenges we face. Let's gather samples and document their locations. It might provide us with an advantage in understanding their patterns and potential weaknesses," Dr. Carter added.

The team carefully collects samples of the scattered minerals and gems, documenting their findings as they continue their journey through the tunnel. The team tenses up at the chilling clicking sound, their hearts racing in their chests. Dr. Ivanov adjusts his grip on his flashlight, his knuckles turning white. The sergeant motions for everyone to halt, signaling for silence. The echoes of their footsteps fade away, leaving an eerie stillness in the air. They strain their ears, listening intently for any further indication of movement.

The clicking sound grows louder, closer. Then, from the shadows, the faint glint of multiple pairs of luminescent eyes catches their attention. The team's flashlights illuminate the grotesque forms of the spiders, emerging from hidden crevices and descending from above. Reacting swiftly, the sergeant barks out orders. "Fire at will! Aim for their weak spots! Watch out for their mandibles!" Gunfire erupts once again, illuminating the chamber with muzzle flashes. The spiders retaliate with alarming agility, lunging towards the team members with their venomous fangs poised to strike.

Dr. Carter swiftly moves to a vantage point, analyzing the spiders' behavior, searching for vulnerabilities. "Their abdomen! Aim for their abdomen! It's a potential weak spot!" she shouts, her voice cutting through the chaos. The team adjusts their aim, directing their firepower towards the identified target. Explosions of gunfire and flashes of light fill the chamber as the team fights back with determination and precision. The spiders, although formidable, are not invincible. Each well-placed shot and explosive strike weakens their onslaught. The team's expertise and coordination begin to turn the tide of the battle.

But the spiders are relentless, their numbers seemingly endless. The team's ammunition dwindles, and exhaustion threatens to take its toll. They need a breakthrough, a decisive action to tip the scales in their favor. Dr. Ivanov, his eyes scanning the chamber, notices a pattern in the spiders' movements. "There! The ceiling! They seem to be descending from above. If we can disrupt their entry points, we may have a chance!"

With a newfound sense of purpose, the team focuses their efforts on targeting the openings in the cave's ceiling, where the spiders emerge. Grenades and well-aimed shots are directed towards these vulnerable spots, causing debris to rain down and obstruct the spiders' access.As the chamber fills with smoke and dust, the team seizes the opportunity to reposition and regroup. They take advantage of the chaos to catch their breath and formulate a new plan of attack.

Dr. Carter, her mind racing, suggests, "We need to use the environment to our advantage. Let's create chokepoints and set up traps. If we can bottleneck their movements, it will give us the upper hand." The team springs into action, strategically placing obstacles and setting traps along the spiders' anticipated paths. Improvised barriers, tripwires, and snares are skillfully deployed, designed to hinder and incapacitate the creatures.

With their defenses fortified, the team readies themselves for the next wave of spiders. Tension fills the chamber as they wait, their fingers twitching on the triggers, prepared to unleash their firepower. The battle resumes, the team engaging the spiders with renewed vigor and a calculated strategy. Each member plays their part, their expertise combining to create a formidable force. The spiders, caught off guard by the team's defensive measures, struggle to navigate the treacherous terrain.

As the fight rages on, the tide gradually turns in favor of the team. The spiders' numbers dwindle, their movements becoming more desperate and disorganized. The team's relentless assault pushes them back, inch by inch, reclaiming control of the chamber. Finally, with a final surge of determination, the team delivers the decisive blow. The last remaining spiders are defeated, their lifeless forms scattered across the chamber floor. Exhausted but triumphant, the team takes a moment to catch their breath and assess the aftermath of the battle.

Dr. Ivanov wipes the sweat from his brow, a mixture of relief and pride in his eyes. "We did it. We held our ground and fought back. But this is just the beginning. We must continue our efforts to understand and eliminate this threat." The team nods in agreement, their resolve unwavering.

Back at the main tent, Dr. Williams, Dr. Stevenson, and General Hargrove anxiously await the return of the second team, concern etched on their faces. The atmosphere in the tent is heavy with the weight of loss. With a voice heavy with sorrow, General Hargrove addresses the shaken group. "We've lost more good men. They fought bravely, and their sacrifice will not be forgotten." General Hargrove, Dr. Williams, and Dr. Stevenson gather around a large map, exhaustion and grief evident in their eyes. Dr. Williams reexamines her drawing.

Dr. Carter's group makes it back to the tent and joins the first group showing them the samples they collected. Dr. Williams approaches the General. "General, these tunnels are interconnected, linking this cave to the other structures we've encountered. And it seems they all converge with the Kola borehole." General Hargrove comes out of his deep thought.

"So, they've been using this extensive underground network to move undetected and establish their presence throughout the area." Dr. Williams nods in agreement.

"Yes, General. It appears that these creatures have been utilizing the underground network as a means of travel and expansion. It explains their ability to emerge and retreat swiftly, evading our detection until now. The interconnected nature of these tunnels poses a significant challenge in eradicating their presence completely."

General Hargrove's expression grows serious as he considers the implications. "If they have established such an extensive network, it means our fight extends far beyond the surface. We need to devise a comprehensive strategy that targets not only the creatures on the ground but also disrupts their underground operations."

Dr. Stevenson adds, "We may need to explore methods of collapsing or sealing off these underground tunnels, preventing the creatures from freely moving between them and limiting their ability to expand further. It won't be an easy task, but it could be a crucial step in weakening their foothold."

The team begins to brainstorm, combining their scientific knowledge and military expertise to formulate a plan of action. They discuss the potential use of explosives, controlled cave-ins, and sealing techniques to disrupt the creatures' movements underground. Their goal is not only to neutralize the immediate threat but to dismantle their infrastructure and cut off their means of expansion.

Dr. Stevenson, with eyes wide open with understanding, looked at everyone. "If we can unravel the labyrinthine system and understand their movements within it, we may find a way to strike at their core."

"Agreed. We need a comprehensive plan to secure and map out the entire network," General Hargrove said with authority.

"Sorry. I don't think that will help. Look at my drawing again. All these caves connect with the Kola borehole. It's like they branch off a main line like a passenger train. But these creatures have the unique ability to bore into another section rapidly if a section or tunnel collapses or is blocked. Even if we map out the whole cave system, they will just create a whole new network.

General Hargrove studies the drawing once again, his brow furrowed with deep concern. Dr. Carter and Dr. Stevenson exchange worried glances as they absorb the implications of the interconnected cave system.

General Hargrove, obviously frustrated, looked directly at Dr. Williams, "You're right. Mapping out the existing cave system won't be enough. These creatures possess an adaptive capability that allows them to rapidly create new tunnels. We need to concentrate on the borehole."

Dr. Williams looks up after examining the samples brought back by the second team. "Based on my analysis, these minerals and gems can help us track the creatures' movements and potentially identify key areas in their tunnel network."

"I don't follow you. How can a bunch of rocks help it?" the general asked.

Dr. Carter smiles. "What Dr. Williams is alluding to is that we need to map out the mineral deposits and cross-reference them with the cave network. It could give us insights into their migration patterns and potentially reveal vulnerable points in their tunnel system."

Dr. Williams sets up her laptop, connecting it to a projector, and begins analyzing the geological striations for the region. The team gathers around, their eyes fixed on the screen as she navigates through the data. "Take a look, everyone. These geological striations depict the layers of rock formations in the area, extending down to the depth reached by the Kola Superdeep borehole."

As the team examines the visual representation of the geological data, a pattern emerges, capturing their attention. "Look at this! The samples taken by Dr. Carter's team match a specific geological layer, approximately halfway to the depth of the borehole."

"Exactly," an excited Dr. Stevenson said, looking back and forth between the picture on the screen and Dr. Williams. "Exactly. If these samples originated from that depth, it suggests that the creatures' original nesting and their home base might be in that area."

General Hargrove concurs. "That's a significant discovery. If we can pinpoint their original nest, we can launch a targeted offensive and eliminate the threat at its source."

Dr. Williams nods, her excitement palpable. "Indeed, General. By studying the geological data and the mineral composition of the samples, we can narrow down the potential location of the creatures' nest. This will allow us to focus our resources and efforts on a precise strike, maximizing our chances of success."

General Hargrove stands near the entrance of the main tent, peering out into the raging Arctic storm. The wind howls at incredible speeds, whipping snow and ice through the air. The temperature drops rapidly, turning the surroundings into a frozen, unforgiving landscape. With a strained voice he addresses the group. "This storm... It's more powerful than we anticipated. The conditions out there are treacherous." He watches as the storm intensifies, the fury of nature on full display.

Inside the tent, the scientists and remaining soldiers huddle together, seeking warmth and shelter from the brutal elements. The sound of the wind rattling the tent echoes through the space. Finally General Hargrove broke the silence. "We need to ensure the camp's stability. The tents, equipment, and our defenses must withstand this storm."

Dr. Carter nods in agreement. "We can't afford any weak points. The storm could be as dangerous as the spiders themselves." The group springs into action, reinforcing the tent structures, securing equipment, and fortifying the defenses. Their very survival depends on their preparations.

The storm showed no signs of letting up. It raged with unrelenting force. Snow and ice whip through the air, creating a blinding whiteout. Visibility is reduced to mere feet. The soldiers brave the elements, battling against the howling winds and icy onslaught. They secure the perimeter, ensuring that their defenses hold strong against both the storm and potential spider attacks.

Dr. Ivanov notices the grim look on most people's faces. "We've faced countless challenges already. We can't let this storm be our downfall. Our determination will see us through. Remember the Soviets' gallant stand against the Nazis at Stalingrad."

Dusk arrives. The team gathers closer, finding strength in each other as they await the storm's passing. Suddenly, sporadic explosions resonate through the air, originating from different locations across the Kola site. The ground rumbles as if in response to the creatures' relentless attempts to emerge from their underground caves. Soldiers stationed at various points around the site respond swiftly, their weapons ready to repel any breach.

One soldier's voice is heard shouting. "They're trying to break through! Hold the line! Don't let them escape!" The soldiers stand their ground, unleashing a barrage of firepower against the creatures' onslaught. The night sky flickers with the glow of muzzle flashes and the sound of explosions reverberates through the frigid air.

Another soldier admonishes the others. "They won't get past us but use the grenades sparingly." Despite the ferocity of the creatures' attacks, the soldiers hold their position, determined to protect the camp from the impending threat.

The group withstands another assault by the creatures who retreat at the morning sunrise. The soldiers stand firm, braving the freezing temperatures and violent winds. A tense calm settles over the camp. The soldiers and the scientists catch their breath, surveying the aftermath of the battle.

As daylight continues to pierce through the clouds, casting a pale light over the camp. Dr. Williams observes the ongoing storm, deep in thought. She notices a pattern emerging from their encounters with the creatures. "There's a consistent pattern to their attacks." Everyone including the soldiers and General Hargrove turn their attention to Dr. Williams. "They only seem to strike during the night. Even with this storm, they avoid daylight at all costs."

"Yes," Dr. Ivanov states. "It's as if they have an aversion to sunlight. Perhaps they possess a biological sensitivity to daylight, like certain nocturnal creatures."

"If that's the case, it could be a weakness we can exploit. Sunlight appears to render them vulnerable or inhibit their movements," Dr. Stevenson contributed.

"I'll analyze our data and look for any supporting evidence. If we can find a way to harness the power of daylight against them, it could turn the tide in our favor," Dr. Williams said. Excitedly, Dr. Williams and Dr. Stevenson meticulously review their research, pouring over data and maps, searching for clues to confirm their daylight hypothesis.

Dr. Williams nods in agreement, her eyes shining with determination. "Yes, General. We need to be proactive and prepared for any situation. With a well-planned network of powerful lighting, we can create a perimeter of safety that will deter the creatures from approaching our camp. It will buy us time and ensure our defenses remain strong."

Dr. Stevenson adds, "Additionally, we can utilize certain wavelengths of light that are known to disrupt arachnid behavior. By incorporating those into our lighting setup, we can further discourage the creatures from venturing near our camp."

General Hargrove acknowledges their suggestions with a firm nod. "Excellent ideas, both of you. Make it happen. I want our camp illuminated like never before. Mobilize the troops and assign them to set up the lighting system immediately. We can't afford to waste any more time."

The soldiers spring into action, swiftly organizing the placement of floodlights, spotlights, and other lighting equipment throughout the camp. The powerful beams of light pierce the darkness, creating a bright barrier of protection that stretches far into the surrounding area.

As the lights are set up, the team takes a moment to observe the transformation. The once dark and foreboding campsite now stands bathed in a brilliant glow, a testament to their ingenuity and resourcefulness. Dr. Williams and Dr. Stevenson exchange a look of satisfaction. Their plan is in motion, and they are confident that the combination of artificial light and disrupted arachnid behavior will significantly enhance the camp's defense against the creatures.

The lighting system proves to be an effective deterrent. The creatures keep their distance, avoiding the brightly lit perimeter of the camp. The soldiers and scientists can now focus on regrouping, reinforcing their defenses, and preparing for the arrival of reinforcements.

The storm has blanketed the region in snow. The camp remains aglow, immune to the encroaching darkness. The powerful floodlights and spotlights continue to pierce through the storm, ensuring the camp remains a beacon of safety. The creatures, unable to find the cover of darkness they seek, remain at bay, their attempts to approach the camp thwarted by the continuous illumination. The combination of artificial light and disrupted behavior proves to be a winning strategy.

Dr. Ivanov recommended that they need to establish a backup power system to sustain the lighting equipment in case the storm affects our primary power supply. General Hargrove nods in agreement. "Agreed. We'll prioritize securing alternative power sources, such as generators and battery packs, to ensure our defenses remain operational under any circumstances. Time is of the essence. Dusk is approaching."

Dr. Williams and Dr. Stevenson immediately set to work, coordinating with the soldiers to secure generators and battery packs. They strategically position these backup power sources throughout the camp, ensuring that the lighting system remains fully functional even in the face of a power outage.

As dusk descends upon the camp, the storm intensifies, and darkness envelopes the surroundings. The primary power supply is tested, but the backup power system seamlessly kicks in, illuminating the camp once again. The powerful floodlights and spotlights cut through the stormy night, creating a safe haven amidst the raging elements.

The soldiers stand guard, their eyes scanning the perimeter, ready to defend against any potential threat. The constant hum of the generators provides a comforting reassurance, knowing that the lights will not falter and the camp's defenses will remain strong. Some spiders attempt to carve out exits in the snow mounds, but once they complete the opening, immediately retreat due to the intense light.

Inside the command tent, General Hargrove monitors the situation, closely observing the radar and communication systems. He feels a sense of confidence knowing that their preparations have paid off. The backup power system ensures that the camp's defenses remain operational, providing a vital advantage against the creatures.

Dr. Williams and Dr. Stevenson join General Hargrove in the command tent, their faces reflecting a mix of exhaustion and relief. They exchange glances, knowing that their collective efforts have paid off. The storm rages on, testing the resolve of everyone in the camp. But with the powerful lighting system and the backup power supply, the creatures are still being kept at bay. Their attempts to breach the camp's perimeter are met with a wall of light and an unwavering defense.

Dr. Stevenson watches and sees the spiders trying to breach the security now put in place. "The lighting seems to be holding them at bay. They're avoiding the illuminated areas."

"Yes, it's working," Dr. Carter says excitedly. "We're successfully using artificial light as a deterrent."

"Remember however, that these sneaky bastards will now start to burrow other tunnels probing for an exit. General, you must alert your soldiers to be on alert for new cave-like structures," Dr. Williams said with a stern look on her face.

Inside the main tent, the team keeps a close eye on the storm's progress. They stand ready to activate the backup lighting system if needed. General Hargrove addresses the exhausted team, emphasizing the need for rest and creating a shift schedule. "Look men, we're all exhausted. We must prioritize our rest to ensure we're fresh and alert during the night. I've created a shift schedule for each of you." He looks at the scientist. "I suggest you do the same." The scientists exchange glances, acknowledging the importance of rest in their current situation.

Dr. Carter volunteers. "I'll take care of the schedule for our team. We'll ensure everyone gets adequate rest while maintaining our defenses General."

After a few minutes of silence, Dr. Stevenson broke the silence and shared his thoughts. "Although our current plan has succeeded in containing the spiders, we mustn't forget that it's only a temporary solution. We still need to locate their central base of operations and devise a strategy to either eradicate them entirely or permanently secure the area."

Dr. Williams agreed, responding, "You're absolutely right. I believe the key to finding their home lies at the midpoint of the Kola hole, where the gems are located. My intuition tells me that's where they originate from. If we can reach that location and trigger a controlled explosion, we have a better chance of eliminating a significant portion of the colony."

Expressing doubt, General Hargrove questioned, "Do spiders really live in colonies? I always thought they were solitary creatures." Everyone turned to Dr. Stevenson, awaiting his response.

"While it is true that most spiders are solitary and even display aggression towards their own kind, there are certain species that exhibit a tendency to live in groups, forming colonies," Dr. Stevenson explained. "Emily's hypothesis is quite plausible. By targeting their colony, we can bring an end to our adversarial spider problem."

With a shrug of his shoulders, General Hargrove acknowledged, "If annihilating their colony is the solution, then that must become our top priority. We should begin preparations for descending into the Kola hole and locating their central base."

The team comprising Drs. Williams, Carter, and Stevenson gathered near the entrance of the Kola Borehole, preparing themselves for the perilous descent into the depths. They were accompanied by General Hargrove and a group of eight soldiers. Each member carried backpacks filled with essential equipment and carried light sources to fend off the lurking spiders. Meanwhile, Dr. Ivanov remained at the base camp, diligently monitoring the team's progress through the radio.

Just before entering the borehole, General Hargrove addressed the group one final time, his voice stern and commanding. "Attention, everyone. Our mission is clear: reach the midpoint of the Kola hole and locate the spiders' home base. As we descend, it is crucial to maintain constant communication and keep our light sources ready at all times. Your tracking devices and our progress is being monitored by Dr. Ivanov. Stay vigilant and never lose sight of our objective. We cannot anticipate the condition of the terrain below, so watch the walls and the ceiling closely. They may have created lateral tunnels. Alright, let's proceed."

"General, may I interject with one more suggestion?" Dr. Williams didn't wait for a response. "We should maintain a safe distance between each other, ensuring optimal light coverage and minimizing the risk of unexpected attacks."

"You all heard the doctor. Let's proceed," General Hargrove affirmed, acknowledging Dr. Williams' input.

Dr. Williams turned to Dr. Stevenson, a clear bond evident between them. "Paul, you know we are all relying on your expertise on the spiders' behavior. I'm staying as close to you as possible."

"I like that," Paul replied.

The team initiated their descent into the dim and constricted corridors of the Kola Borehole. With caution, they skillfully navigated through the unknown territory, relying on their headlamps and supplementary portable light sources to illuminate the path ahead. Even though everyone was carrying a tracking device, General Hargrove wanted to maintain communication with Dr. Ivanov through the radio.

"No signs of activity in this section," General Hargrove reported, relaying the information to Dr. Ivanov. "We will continue moving deeper into the borehole." Dr. Ivanov diligently monitored the team's progress on his laptop, aided by the tracking devices that the General had ensured everyone was equipped with.

"Understood. Please proceed with caution," Dr. Ivanov responded, aware of the potential dangers that lay ahead. The team continued their meticulous navigation through the intricate tunnels, their senses heightened and ready to defend themselves if need be. They advanced methodically, thoroughly examining each crevice and corner in search of any signs or remnants left behind by the spiders.

Eventually, the team arrived at a junction where two main tunnels diverged. General Hargrove made the decision to divide their forces. He selected two soldiers to explore cavern B while he, along with the remaining members of the group, proceeded into cavern A. This strategic approach allowed them to cover more ground and increase their chances of locating the spiders' home base.

"It feels cooler in here," Dr. Carter observed, sensing a change in temperature within the chamber.

Dr. Stevenson chimed in, noting the distinct difference in the walls' texture. "You're right. The walls appear smoother and more refined, as if they were intentionally constructed—perhaps by the spiders themselves."

As the group continued their exploration, it didn't take long for General Hargrove to halt their advance. "Look," he exclaimed, pointing out a partially concealed, substantial metal door. Recognizing the significance of this discovery, General Hargrove turned to two soldiers. "Breach this door," he commanded, entrusting them with the task.

The soldiers scrutinized the door, deliberating on the appropriate amount of explosives needed for the job. With the decision made, everyone stepped back, preparing for the impending blast. Soon, the soldiers joined the group, cautioning everyone to brace themselves. In a moment of deafening explosion, accompanied by swirling dust and falling debris, the door was blown open, revealing what lay beyond.

General Hargrove, accompanied by Dr. Stevenson, Dr. Williams, Dr. Carter, and the remaining soldiers, cautiously ventured into the expansive, abandoned laboratory concealed within the depths beyond the breached metal door. The space was littered with remnants of scientific apparatus and weathered documents, evoking an air of mystery and intrigue. Navigating through the dimly lit area, the group relied on their flashlights to illuminate their path.

General Hargrove urged everyone to proceed with utmost caution, emphasizing the importance of gathering as much information as possible about the hidden facility. Meanwhile, Dr. Carter's excitement peaked as he discovered numerous glass vials containing preserved specimens of spiders in various stages of development.

Dr. Stevenson joined Dr. Carter in examining the vials, carefully peering into each one with a blend of curiosity and concern. "It's evident that this laboratory was dedicated to studying the spiders. But what was the purpose behind it?" he pondered aloud.

In a hushed tone, as if uncovering a secret, Dr. Williams responded, "The Russians haven't been entirely truthful with us, have they?" The revelation hinted at a hidden agenda and raised questions about the true nature of the spider research conducted within the facility.

"No, they certainly haven't," General Hargrove responded, his tone tinged with disappointment. "We must uncover the complete extent of their involvement and understand the true intentions behind these experiments." Determined to shed light on the matter, the team pressed on, delving deeper into their investigation of the laboratory.

As they explored further, the group came across scattered documents and notes strewn across nearby workstations. Dr. Stevenson's keen eye caught sight of a stack of faded papers, compelling him to pick them up and examine them with great care. With a mixture of intrigue and caution, he delved into the contents, hoping to unravel the secrets concealed within the worn pages.

"These documents unveil a series of genetic studies, behavioral analyses, and the impact of different substances on the spiders. It appears that extensive experimentation was conducted on them," Dr. Stevenson reported, his voice laden with intrigue and concern. He proceeded to gather another stack of documents, eager to uncover more information.

Dr. Williams, perplexed by the revelations, voiced the pressing questions that occupied their thoughts. "But why keep all of this a secret? And what implications does it hold for our mission to contain the spiders?" he inquired, seeking clarification from Dr. Stevenson.

In response, Dr. Stevenson shrugged his shoulders and raised his eyebrows, conveying a mix of uncertainty and curiosity. The full ramifications of the hidden research and its impact on their mission remained shrouded in mystery, leaving them with a sense of urgency to uncover the truth.

"We need to address this hidden laboratory with Dr. Ivanov once we resurface. It appears there is more at stake than we initially realized," General Hargrove asserted, breaking the tense silence. The group exchanged concerned glances, grappling with the weighty implications of their discoveries.

Dr. Williams positioned herself beside Dr. Stevenson, standing united. "Regardless of the intentions behind this research, our primary goal remains halting the destructive rampage of these spiders. We can address the Russian involvement once we have contained the threat," she stated resolutely.

"I concur," General Hargrove agreed, his tone determined. "Let's maintain our focus on the mission at hand but be prepared for any further surprises that may arise." With that, the group departed from the laboratory, retracing their steps back to the junction where the two caverns met, where they were greeted by the soldiers who had just arrived.

"General, sir," an excited soldier exclaimed, unable to contain his astonishment. "You won't believe what we found. There's a massive chamber, and it's occupied by the largest spider I've ever seen."

Upon hearing this, the team advanced, following the soldiers who took the lead. They cautiously proceeded into the expansive chamber; its walls intricately adorned with voluminous webs. Aware of the potential danger, they maintained a safe distance from the webs as they carefully surveyed the surroundings.

"Be cautious to avoid any contact with the cobwebs. It may trigger signals alerting the spiders to our presence," Dr. Stevenson ordered, emphasizing the need for caution. The sheer size and scale of the webs indicated a significant spider presence within the chamber, further creating an apprehension among the team.

Dr. Williams posed a question, seeking confirmation from Dr. Stevenson. "Considering the size and extent of this chamber, could it indicate a large spider population and a nearby central hub?" Dr. Stevenson, though silent, nodded in agreement.

General Hargrove relayed the discovery to Dr. Ivanov via the radio. "Dr. Ivanov, we've stumbled upon what appears to be a network of tunnels leading deeper into the earth. It might be the pathway to their main nest."

Acknowledging the information, Dr. Ivanov responded, "Understood. I've marked the location." Encouraged by this acknowledgment, the team cautiously proceeded into the largest chamber they had encountered thus far. The atmosphere grew heavy and steamy, creating a warm and stifling ambiance. As they ventured deeper into the chamber, their attention was drawn to a colossal web structure and an unsettling pulsating sound, further heightening the tension in the air.

"Look at the sheer size of this chamber. It's absolutely massive," Dr. Williams exclaimed in awe, taking in the expansive surroundings. Dr. Stevenson's voice was filled with a mix of concern and intrigue as he observed the environment. "The temperature is rising, creating a natural incubator of sorts. Something significant is transpiring in this area."

As the team continued their exploration, their eyes widened in astonishment as they came face-to-face with the queen spider. Towering above them, the queen surpassed the size of any spider they had encountered before. She was engrossed in the vital task of laying eggs, attended to by a swarm of smaller spiders dutifully tending to her.

Fixated on the enormous creature, Dr. Stevenson declared with certainty, "Without a doubt, this is the queen. She is colossal—a formidable source of their reproduction and power." The team stood in awe of this remarkable discovery, realizing the critical role the queen played in the spiders' hierarchy and propagation.

"Maintain your positions, everyone," General Hargrove commanded, his voice firm and composed. "If the queen becomes aware of our presence, the sheer number of spiders in this chamber could overwhelm us." The team froze in place, obediently following the general's orders. They suppressed their breathing, attempting to remain as silent as possible, fully aware that the slightest movement or sound could give away their presence to the other spiders lurking nearby.

The queen spider, sensing a disturbance, shifted its massive form, indicating its heightened awareness of something amiss in the chamber. In a hushed but audible tone, Dr. Stevenson addressed the team, urging them to remain steady and hidden. Each member pressed themselves against the chamber walls, blending into the shadows, their hearts pounding in their chests. They held their collective breath, fervently hoping that their presence would go undetected, praying for the moment to pass without incident.

The queen emitted a low rumble, her numerous eyes scanning the area, searching diligently for any signs of intruders. Suspicion hung in the air as she lingered, unable to pinpoint the exact location of the intruders. After a moment's hesitation, she emitted a final chittering sound before turning away, retreating to another section of the chamber.

A collective sigh of relief swept through the team as Dr. Stevenson took a deep breath. "She's gone... for now," he stated, his voice reflecting a mixture of relief and caution. Recognizing the need to regroup and strategize, he emphasized the importance of proceeding with utmost care.

General Hargrove took the lead, initiating their retreat from the expansive chamber. Moving silently, the team meticulously retraced their steps through the intricate tunnels of the Kola Borehole, each member aware of the delicate nature of their mission and the need for utmost vigilance while retreating from the underground caves.

Gathered together in the main tent, the team's expressions reflected a mixture of determination and weariness. They shared their harrowing encounter with the queen spider, emphasizing the urgency of their next moves. General Hargrove addressed the exhausted group.

"We have witnessed firsthand the immense power and danger the queen spider possesses," General Hargrove began, his tone somber yet resolute. "It is imperative that we gather our strength and devise a meticulous plan for our return to the largest chamber. Our objective remains unchanged: to destroy the queen and eliminate the threat posed by the remaining eggs." He paused, allowing his words to sink in among the team members.

"I completely agree, General," Dr. Williams affirmed. "Approaching this situation with utmost caution is crucial. The queen possesses unique abilities and poses a formidable challenge. We must devise a detailed strategy and ensure we have the right equipment if we are to have a chance at success."

Dr. Stevenson chimed in, adding to the discussion. "I've been closely studying the queen's behavior and analyzing the chamber layout. It is evident that she is not only highly territorial but also fiercely protective of her eggs. We should exploit this weakness to our advantage."

General Hargrove, curious about the proposed approach, inquired, "And how do we accomplish that, Doctor? Charging in with guns blazing proved ineffective during our initial encounter."

A smile crept onto Dr. Stevenson's face as he responded to the General's question. "No, General, that would indeed be reckless. Instead, we'll employ a strategy of distraction and deception. By creating a convincing enough threat elsewhere in the chamber, we can lure the queen away from her nest. Her instinct to defend her territory will lead her away from the eggs, allowing us an opportunity to strike."

The team nodded in agreement, recognizing the importance of using cunning and strategy to outwit the queen spider. Their plan began to take shape, fueled by a combination of scientific analysis and tactical expertise. They understood that their success relied not only on their individual skills but also on their ability to work together, leveraging the queen's weaknesses against her in a calculated and strategic manner.

Dr. Stevenson paused for a moment, considering the General's question. However, before he could respond, Dr. Williams stepped in, presenting a holographic map for everyone to see.

"Take a look," Dr. Williams said, pointing to the map. "There's a subterranean lake not far from the chamber. I propose engineering an artificial seismic event, simulating an earthquake. The resulting vibrations and sound should trigger the queen's instincts to protect her eggs. During her moment of vulnerability, we can position ourselves strategically to launch our attack."

General Hargrove nodded in agreement, fully understanding the significance of the plan. "Make it happen, Doctors," he said, his voice resolute. "We need a detailed plan and must utilize every resource at our disposal. Lives are at stake, and we cannot afford any more losses. Let us prepare for this mission with the utmost diligence."

The team nods in agreement, their determination renewed. They disperse, each member taking up their respective tasks to prepare for the daring mission ahead. Darkness returns. As the team finalizes their plan, the storm outside intensifies, the wind howling and rain pouring down heavily. The sound of thunder echoes in the distance, adding an eerie atmosphere to their already tense situation. They exchange glances, knowing that time is of the essence.

The General must raise his voice to be heard over the storm. "We can't afford any more delays. Gather your gear and prepare to re-enter the borehole. Move swiftly but stay alert. We don't know what else may be lurking down there. The team quickly readies themselves, checking their weapons and equipment one last time. They start their descent into the borehole. Just then a deafening shriek pierces the air. They turn in horror to see a massive spider lunging partially out of the hole at the first soldier, its fangs sinking into his flesh and then throwing the soldier towards a wall.

The team's initial response is swift and coordinated, a flurry of gunfire and a well-aimed grenade aimed at the attacking spider. The explosion tears through the creature, shattering its body and scattering its remnants throughout the chamber. The acrid smell of burning flesh fills the air as the team takes a moment to assess the aftermath.

With the immediate threat neutralized, the doctors, rushed to provide medical assistance to the fallen soldier. However, it becomes apparent that their efforts are in vain as the soldier's condition rapidly deteriorates. Violent spasms wrack his body, and despite the doctors' best attempts, it becomes clear that he cannot be saved. The team is left in a state of shock and sorrow, grappling with the sudden loss of their comrade.

Silence settles over the chamber as the weight of the soldier's sacrifice sinks in. Each member of the team processes the tragedy in their own way, mourning the loss of a valued ally and friend. It serves as a stark reminder of the dangers they face and the sacrifices they must make in their mission to protect others.

In the aftermath, the team regroups, their determination fueled by the memory of their fallen comrade. They push forward, resolved to complete their mission and honor the soldier's sacrifice.

With a heavy heart, Hargrove takes charge, his face etched with determination despite the somber atmosphere. The team understands and follows his lead, knowing that time is of the essence. They press forward, cautiously navigating the intricate tunnels that stretch deeper into the bowels of the earth.

As they make their way, a stroke of luck befalls them. The ongoing storm outside creates a symphony of thunder and rain, effectively muffling any noise the team might be generating. They silently acknowledge this stroke of fortune, knowing that it may have shielded their approach from the keen senses of the spiders.

Reaching a predetermined point, the team splits into two groups. Dr. Carter, accompanied by a contingent of soldiers, ventures toward the subterranean lake, their mission to set up the explosive device. They understood their task and proceeded with caution, aware that any misstep could spell disaster.

General Hargrove takes the lead of the remaining group, composed of Drs. Williams and Stevenson. Their destination lies deeper within the labyrinthine tunnels—the queen's chamber. With each step, their anticipation grows, mingled with a sense of trepidation. The stakes are high, but they carry the weight of their fallen comrade's sacrifice as a constant reminder.

Their path winds through winding tunnels, occasionally illuminated by the faint glow of phosphorescent fungi clinging to the damp walls. The silence is broken only by the sound of their breathing and the distant rumble of thunder, echoing through the earth.

As they delve deeper into the subterranean realm, the air grows thick with anticipation. The team knows they are drawing closer to the heart of the spider menace—the queen herself. With each step, they prepare themselves mentally and physically for the battle ahead, their resolve unyielding.

Finally, after what feels like an eternity, they arrive at the entrance to the queen's chamber—a massive, sprawling cavern enveloped in darkness. General Hargrove shares a steely glance with his comrades, and without a word, they step into the unknown, ready to face whatever horrors await them and bring an end to this nightmare once and for all.

Dr. Carter's group cautiously makes their way to the designated spot where the explosive device is to be placed. With a firm gesture, she instructs a soldier to position it, ensuring it is strategically located for maximum impact. The soldier follows her orders, handling the explosive with utmost care, aware of the importance of their mission.

As the device is set in place, Dr. Carter addresses the team, "We must move quickly once this is set off. The resulting vibrations and noise will draw the queen away from her nest, giving us a chance to reach a safe distance." The soldiers listen attentively, their eyes scanning their surroundings, senses heightened for any signs of danger. Each member of the group understands the critical role they play in the success of the mission.

With everything in place, the team braces themselves, mentally preparing for what lies ahead. Each member understands that timing is crucial; they must execute their plan flawlessly to ensure their own safety and maximize their chances of success.

Dr. Carter gives a nod of affirmation, signaling the moment they have been waiting for. The soldier responsible for triggering the explosive steps back, activating the device with a steady hand. A tense silence hangs in the air for a brief moment before the chamber reverberates with a deafening blast.

The ground shakes, and the noise echoes through the tunnels, reaching the queen's sensitive senses. The team wastes no time, swiftly retreating to a safe distance, knowing that the commotion will draw the queen away from her nest. Their hearts race with anticipation as they anticipate the imminent confrontation with the massive arachnid and the challenges it will present.

With the explosive detonated and their part of the plan set in motion, Dr. Carter's group joins forces with General Hargrove's team, converging on a rendezvous point. Together, they will face the final leg of their mission—the decisive battle against the queen and her brood.

The queen, startled by the explosive blast and the reverberations that shake her chamber, reacts with a mix of instinctual fury and maternal protectiveness. Sensing a danger to her precious eggs, she abandons her position, abandoning the comfort and security of her nest. With each calculated movement, she ventures deeper into the labyrinthine tunnels, her massive form causing the very earth to tremble.

Driven by an intense urge to defend her offspring, the queen follows the vibrations and noise, her chitinous limbs propelling her forward with a frightening agility. The darkness of the tunnels serves as a backdrop to her relentless pursuit, her keen senses attuned to any hint of the intruders who dared to disturb her domain.

Meanwhile, Dr. Carter's group, now united with General Hargrove and the other members of their team, cautiously advances, their footsteps echoing through the now-deserted chamber. The tension is palpable as they press forward, aware that the queen is on the move and drawing nearer with every passing moment.

The team moves swiftly, adrenaline coursing through their veins, as they navigate the labyrinthine network of tunnels. Their goal is clear—to confront the queen, eliminate the threat once and for all, and ensure the safety of those who remain vulnerable to the arachnid menace.

As they proceed, the sound of scuttling echoes in the distance, growing louder and more menacing with each passing step. Shadows dance on the walls, hinting at the queen's imminent arrival. The team readies themselves, weapons at the ready, their resolve unwavering.

Finally, in the dim light ahead, they catch a glimpse of the queen—a gargantuan arachnid, her multifaceted eyes gleaming with a mixture of aggression and maternal instinct. The queen stops momentarily, sensing the presence of her adversaries. A tense standoff ensues as the team faces off against this formidable creature, aware that their mission hangs in the balance.

With hearts pounding, the team engages in a battle of survival, unleashing a barrage of firepower and strategic maneuvers against the queen spider. They must rely on their training, their unity as a team, and their unwavering determination to overcome this colossal adversary.

The chamber reverberates with the clash of metal and the sound of gunfire. The team fights valiantly, never losing sight of their mission—to protect and save lives. Their every move is calculated, each action infused with a sense of purpose.

Dr. Stevenson, caught up in the excitement of their plan working, turns to Dr. Williams with a glimmer of hope in his eyes. "It's working! She's on the move," he exclaims, his voice filled with a mixture of excitement and relief. In a moment of spontaneous emotion, he leans in and plants a kiss on her forehead, a gesture fueled by the adrenaline and the shared intensity of the situation.

As soon as the realization of his action sinks in, Dr. Stevenson's cheeks flush with embarrassment.

He quickly averts his gaze, momentarily at a loss for words, realizing the inappropriate nature of his gesture in such a critical moment. Dr. Williams, for her part, is taken aback by the unexpected display of affection but manages to maintain her composure, understanding the context in which it occurred.

Aware of the need to refocus their attention, both Dr. Stevenson and Dr. Williams take cover behind a rocky outcrop, positioning themselves strategically to keep a vigilant watch on the entrance of the chamber. They regain their professional composure, fully aware that their primary objective is to remain alert and ready for any sign of the queen's return.

The remaining soldiers stand beside them, their eyes scanning the surroundings, their weapons held firmly, their resolve unyielding. The team is poised and prepared, awaiting further orders from General Hargrove, who remains composed, his gaze fixed on the chamber's entrance.

Time seems to stretch as they maintain their positions, their breath held in anticipation. Each passing moment heightens the tension, their senses attuned to the slightest sound or movement that could signify the queen's return. The weight of the mission bears down on them, reminding them of the stakes at hand.

Minutes pass, seemingly dragging on indefinitely. The air grows thick with anticipation, but they know that patience is key. They must wait for the right moment, the perfect opportunity to strike and neutralize the queen once and for all.

In the midst of this tense silence, the team's shared camaraderie and dedication to their cause bind them together. The memory of their fallen comrade lingers, reminding them of the sacrifice that has brought them to this point. They draw strength from each other, forming an unbreakable bond that fuels their determination to see the mission through to its conclusion.

With eyes fixed on the entrance, hearts pounding with anticipation, the team remains vigilant, ready to seize the moment when the queen returns, to confront her head-on, and to bring an end to the nightmare that has plagued them and threatened the lives of countless others.

Deep within the convoluted network of tunnels, the queen roams, her movements guided by a potent mix of instinct and maternal protectiveness. Her colossal legs send tremors through the earth, each step a testament to her relentless determination.

As she traverses the labyrinthine passageways, her keen senses detect the lingering vibrations and echoes of the explosive blast. The disturbance fuels her curiosity and triggers a primal response—an overwhelming need to investigate the source of the disruption, as well as a fierce determination to defend her progeny.

With every stride, the queen's massive form weaves through the web-covered tunnels, her many eyes scanning for any signs of intrusion or danger. The maternal instinct within her core drives her forward, her brood's safety being paramount above all else.

Guided by her senses, she follows the remnants of scent and sound, gradually drawing closer to the origin of the disturbance. Her multifaceted eyes, adapted for darkness, pierce through the shadows as she navigates the intricate paths, her chitinous exoskeleton scraping against the rough walls.

Meanwhile, the team, hidden behind the rocky outcrop, remains vigilant, their breaths held in anticipation. They know that the queen's return is imminent, and the next phase of their plan will unfold when she reenters the chamber. Their focus is unwavering, their determination resolute as they await the right moment to strike.

Back in the depths of the tunnels, the queen senses the nearness of her nest. Her maternal instincts intensify, urging her to hasten her pace. Her formidable mandibles twitch with a mix of anticipation and protection, ready to fend off any potential threats to her brood.

Driven by an innate force, the queen spider finally arrives at the entrance of the chamber. Her eight legs bring her to a halt as she surveys the surroundings, her multitude of eyes scanning the chamber's interior. A palpable tension hangs in the air as the team and the queen stand poised on opposite sides, each awaiting the other's next move.

In that moment, a silent battle of wills commences—the team, resolute in their mission to neutralize the queen and eliminate the arachnid menace, and the queen, resolute in her duty to protect her eggs and defend her territory.

The tension in the queen's chamber reaches its peak as the soldiers, Dr. Williams, and Dr. Stevenson remain hidden, nerves on edge, awaiting the queen's return. Minutes pass like an eternity, the air heavy with anticipation, until a subtle shift alerts them—a sign that the queen spider is approaching.

In the dim light, the massive form of the queen becomes visible, her presence casting an ominous shadow over the chamber. General Hargrove whispers urgently to his men, instructing them to hold off on activating the explosives until the queen reaches the center of her egg cluster. The team remains steadfast, ready to execute their plan with precision.

However, their focus is abruptly shattered by piercing screams from Dr. Williams. Their attention diverted, they turn to witness a harrowing scene—baby spiders have swarmed Dr. Williams, crawling up her legs and onto her head. Panic and fear fill the air as the soldiers and Dr. Stevenson react in a race against time to save her.

Reacting swiftly, Dr. Stevenson rushes to Dr. Williams' aid, frantically swatting the baby spiders off her head and legs. Despite his efforts, Dr. Williams receives multiple bites, each venomous sting causing her immense pain. She collapses to the ground, trembling and wracked with agony.

Dr. Stevenson, filled with concern, quickly checks Dr. Williams for acid burns, finding none. The distress calls emitted by the tiny spiders echo through the chamber, capturing the attention of the nearby queen, amplifying her rage.

Enraged by the cries of her offspring, the queen springs into action with alarming speed, her massive form charging toward the soldiers. Her mandibles snap with ferocious intent, venom dripping from her fangs, as she seeks to protect her young and exact revenge upon those who have harmed them.

Aware that time is of the essence, General Hargrove issues a critical command, his voice laced with urgency and resolve. "Fall back! Now!" The soldiers, Dr. Stevenson, and even the injured Dr. Williams quickly heed the order, retreating swiftly and strategically from the queen's path, their survival hanging in the balance.

With every step they take, the chamber reverberates with the queen's enraged pursuit. The team knows they must regroup, find a defensible position, and rally their forces to fend off this formidable adversary. The stakes have never been higher, and their unity and resilience will be tested as they fight for their lives against the vengeful queen spider.

Amidst the chaos and the ferocious screams of the queen, Dr. Stevenson's urgent voice cuts through the commotion, addressing General Hargrove. Dr. Stevenson reveals the severity of Dr. Williams' condition. The venomous bites she has suffered threaten her life, and immediate medical attention is necessary.

Dr. Stevenson emphasizes the need to retreat to the safety of the tent, where he has access to anti-venom. Though unsure of its effectiveness against the spider's potent venom, time is a precious commodity that cannot be wasted. The team's collective focus shifts from battling the queen to securing the wounded and providing the best chance for Dr. Williams' survival.

General Hargrove swiftly responds, barking out orders to the soldiers. The retreat becomes a scramble, a race against the queen's relentless pursuit. Hearts pound in chests as the team distances themselves from the advancing arachnid, desperately seeking a momentary respite to regroup and strategize.

Taking cover behind a rocky outcrop, the soldiers catch their breath, their minds racing to devise a plan. The weight of the situation hangs heavy in the air, a test of their resilience and resourcefulness. Each member of the team, including Dr. Stevenson, contributes their insights and experiences, pooling their collective knowledge to overcome this unforeseen obstacle.

General Hargrove, their unwavering leader, surveys the surroundings, his gaze fixed on the advancing queen spider. He knows that every second counts and that a swift decision must be made. With a firm resolve, he commands the team to hold their ground, weapons poised and ready, as they await further instructions.

Dr. Stevenson, desperate to save Dr. Williams, maintains his focus on the task at hand. He mentally prepares himself for the challenging journey back to the tent, where the anti-venom awaits. Uncertainty lingers but hope fuels his determination to do everything in his power to save his colleague's life.

The queen, her instincts sharpened by rage and protectiveness, closes the distance to the position previously occupied by the soldiers. She skitters forward, her massive legs thudding against the ground, as she searches for the perceived threat to her young.

General Hargrove gives a decisive command to activate the detonation sequence. The soldiers swiftly press the buttons on their detonators, triggering a series of powerful explosions that reverberate through the queen's chamber. The clutch of eggs is obliterated in a fiery blast, the air thick with smoke and debris. The team watches with bated breath, their hopes pinned on the effectiveness of their actions in dealing a significant blow to the queen spider's legacy.

Amidst the chaos, General Hargrove quickly assesses the situation, his concern evident on his face. Dr. Stevenson carries the injured Dr. Williams, her breathing heavy, and visible spider bites mar her arm, face, and neck. The soldiers, hearts pounding in their chests, retreat in a scramble, keeping their weapons at the ready as they distance themselves from the approaching queen spider. They regroup behind a protective rocky outcrop, seeking cover from the looming threat.

In the midst of their hasty retreat, a soldier steps forward, addressing General Hargrove with a suggestion. He proposes exploiting the queen's extreme agitation by leading her into a trap or causing her to lose her balance. The soldier's plan aims to take advantage of the queen's instability, turning it against her.

Another soldier adds to the conversation, suggesting the strategic placement of the remaining explosives at key points. By collapsing parts of the cavern, they hope to trap the queen spider within, limiting her movements and diminishing her advantage.

Dr. Stevenson contributes to the discussion, offering an additional idea. He suggests utilizing fire as a deterrent, as spiders generally have an aversion to flames. Creating controlled burn areas could discourage the queen spider from advancing further, providing an additional layer of defense.

General Hargrove nods, carefully weighing the options presented by his team. Each suggestion carries potential risks and rewards, and he must make a calculated decision. The fate of their mission and the lives of those involved rest on his judgment.

With determination in his eyes, General Hargrove takes a deep breath and issues his orders, outlining a plan that combines elements from the soldiers' suggestions. The team listens intently, knowing that their collective efforts and resourcefulness will be crucial in turning the tide against the queen spider.

Encouraged by the solid plan put forth by his team, General Hargrove takes charge, his voice projecting authority and determination. He acknowledges the importance of buying enough time to retreat and administer the life-saving anti-venom to Dr. Williams. He sets the plan into motion.

The soldiers spring into action, each member knowing their role and executing their tasks with precision. They position the explosives strategically at key points within the chamber, aiming to limit the queen spider's movements and create a potential trap. Simultaneously, they carefully set up controlled fire zones, creating areas where the flickering flames will deter the arachnid and provide a barrier between the team and the advancing threat.

Tension fills the air as the soldiers work swiftly, their movements purposeful and coordinated. Every second counts, and they understand the imminent danger posed by the approaching queen spider. They share a collective understanding of the stakes and the importance of each action they take.

Throughout the process, General Hargrove oversees the preparations, ensuring that everything aligns with the plan. His leadership and calm demeanor help instill confidence in the team, as they draw on their training and experience to execute their tasks flawlessly.

As the final touches are put in place, the team regroups, taking positions and maintaining readiness. They stand united behind the rocky outcrop, their weapons at the ready, fully aware that the next phase of their plan will put their skills and resolve to the ultimate test.

An air of anticipation and determination permeates the chamber as the team awaits General Hargrove's orders. They know that their actions will shape the course of the battle and potentially determine the fate of their mission. Each member stands prepared, their senses heightened, as they brace themselves for the impending confrontation with the queen spider.

General Hargrove raises his voice, commanding the soldiers to set the explosives and light the fires. The team follows his orders with precision, carefully igniting the flames and ensuring the explosives are strategically placed to create a formidable barrier against the queen spider.

However, as the chaos unfolds, the queen becomes engulfed in rage. Thrashing around with unrestrained fury, she unleashes a torrent of spewed acid, filling the cavern with its hissing and corrosive presence.

Reacting swiftly, General Hargrove shouts a warning, ordering the group to take cover and watch out for the acid. In a synchronized motion, they quickly seek refuge behind the protective shield of the rocky outcrop, shielding themselves from the indiscriminate spray of acid. Despite the queen's wild thrashing, their position remains intact, shielding them from the corrosive substance.

Gradually, the queen exhausts herself, her rampage subsiding. The hissing sound of the acid spray diminishes, allowing the group to cautiously emerge from their shelter. They seize the opportunity to regroup and assess the situation, knowing that time is of the essence.

General Hargrove, unwavering in his determination to neutralize the queen, issues another commanding order. His voice rings out with authority, "Detonate the rest of the explosives!" The soldiers act swiftly, activating the remaining explosives in a synchronized motion. The resulting blast reverberates through the cavern, shockwaves rippling through the earth and causing the ground to tremble violently.

The chamber is engulfed in chaos and turmoil, debris flying through the air as the powerful blast shakes the surroundings. The explosive force rocks the queen's domain, potentially disorienting and incapacitating the massive arachnid.

Amidst the aftermath of the explosion, the team regains their footing, seizing the opportunity to retreat while the queen spider is temporarily weakened. General Hargrove leads them with unwavering determination, each member keenly aware that their survival and the success of their mission hinge on their swift and coordinated actions.

With adrenaline coursing through their veins, they move swiftly, using the chaos to their advantage. They navigate through the now-unstable cavern, their senses alert for any signs of the queen's resurgence. Their goal is clear: to escape the immediate danger zone and continue their fight to protect and save lives.

The ceiling above the queen starts to crumble, stones and debris raining down around her. She thrashes and roars, realizing she's being trapped. Dr. Stevenson, General Hargrove, and the soldiers continue to brace themselves against the force of the explosion. Dr. Stevenson shields Dr. Williams who is unconscious. Dust and rubble fill the air as the ceiling collapses, sealing off the entrance to the queen spider's domain.

As the intense blast reverberates through the chamber, the queen spider finds herself trapped in a nightmare of collapsing surroundings. The ceiling above her begins to crumble, stones and debris raining down in a chaotic descent. The once formidable creature thrashes and roars, a desperate realization dawning upon her that she is being ensnared in an inescapable trap.

In the midst of the chaos, Dr. Stevenson, General Hargrove, and the soldiers hold their ground, bracing themselves against the force of the explosion. They withstand the torrent of dust and rubble that fills the air, their determined expressions unwavering.

The ceiling continues to crumble, piece by piece, sealing off the entrance to the queen spider's domain. The once mighty arachnid is now trapped, confined within her own collapsing realm. The debris cascades down, forming a barrier that seals her off from the outside world.

The sounds of the queen's thrashing and roaring gradually fade as the dust settles and silence permeates the chamber. The team, shrouded in the remnants of the chaos, takes a moment to catch their breath, their eyes surveying the scene before them.

With the entrance sealed, the immediate threat of the queen spider is contained, at least for the time being. But they know that danger still lurks, and they must remain vigilant. The task is not yet complete, and their mission to eradicate the arachnid menace is far from over.

Regrouping amidst the aftermath, the team exchanges glances filled with a mix of relief and determination. They understand that they have achieved a significant victory by trapping the queen spider, but they also know that their work is far from done.

In the dimly lit chamber, surrounded by rubble and the remnants of their battle, they steady themselves. Their minds race with thoughts of what lies ahead—the need to secure their position, tend to Dr. Williams' injuries, and plan their next steps. They draw strength from their shared purpose and the knowledge that they have come this far through perseverance and teamwork.

As the dust settles and the chamber remains shrouded in an eerie silence, the team readies themselves for the challenges that lie ahead. With their determination unyielding, they press onward to a small opening allowing them to escape the borehole.

Within the cavern, a tumultuous tempest of falling rocks and debris engulfs the queen spider. Despite her desperate attempts to fight back, her struggles prove futile against the relentless cascade. With one final screech of defiance, the queen spider succumbs to her entrapment, cut off from the outside world.

Dr. Stevenson, General Hargrove, and the soldiers exchange glances of relief, realizing they have successfully sealed off the queen spider. Amid heavy breaths, General Hargrove declares, "We did it. The queen is contained."

However, their jubilation is tempered by the knowledge that this victory is only temporary. They must now prioritize the safe extraction of Dr. Williams and take measures to seal the opening above ground. Their focus turns to her, and to their alarm, they notice foam emanating from her mouth.

"We must hurry," Dr. Stevenson urges.

Navigating the cavern with caution, Dr. Stevenson, General Hargrove, and the soldiers find themselves confronted by a handful of adult spiders. These arachnids, disturbed by the apparent loss of their queen, emerge from the shadows with agitated movements. Their menacing hisses and clicking sounds reverberate through the air, serving as a chilling reminder that the danger is far from over.

General Hargrove swiftly assesses the situation, recognizing the ongoing threat posed by the adult spiders. With a commanding voice, he orders his men,

"Stay focused! The adult spiders remain a formidable danger. Keep your guard up and be prepared."

The soldiers tighten their grips on their weapons, maintaining a vigilant stance as they carefully observe the movements of the agitated arachnids. Each step they take is deliberate, their senses heightened, and their attention solely devoted to the potential attacks from the remaining spiders.

Dr. Stevenson, keeping a close eye on the situation, remains ready to provide assistance if needed. He understands the importance of staying focused amidst the chaos, ensuring the safety of both the team and the injured Dr. Williams. With their resolve unshaken, the team proceeds through the cavern, their movements calculated and coordinated. They maintain a respectful distance from the adult spiders, ready to respond swiftly and decisively to any sign of aggression.

As they press forward, the echoes of hisses and clicks continue to resonate, a constant reminder of the lingering peril. The soldiers maintain their disciplined composure, following General Hargrove's lead, as they work together to navigate the treacherous path and overcome the remaining threat within the cavern.

The cavern becomes a battleground as the spiders launch aggressive assaults, attacking the retreating group with deadly precision. A fierce and desperate battle ensues, with the soldiers fighting valiantly to fend off the relentless spider attacks. However, despite their courage, the spiders prove to be formidable adversaries, striking with lethal force.

In the midst of the chaos, tragedy strikes as three soldiers fall victim to the spider onslaught, succumbing to their injuries. The remaining soldiers, filled with grief but resolute in their mission, continue to defend themselves and push forward, their determination unwavering. Each step they take becomes a hard-fought battle against the pursuing and unrelenting spiders.

Finally, the retreating group reaches an entrance passageway, offering a temporary respite from the spider attacks. They huddle together, panting heavily as they catch their breath, taking a moment to assess the dire situation they find themselves in. Dr. Stevenson, though exhausted, rallies his remaining comrades, shouting with urgency, "We need to keep pushing forward!"

With heavy hearts, the soldiers, still mourning their fallen comrades, gather their strength and prepare to face the ongoing threat. They know that every move forward is fraught with danger and requires unwavering vigilance.

General Hargrove, displaying leadership in the face of adversity, turns to his remaining soldier, conveying a determined order. "Drop whatever hand grenades you have left into that opening, sealing it once and for all."

The soldier, following the command without hesitation, retrieves the remaining hand grenades and tosses them into the entrance of the borehole. Explosions reverberate through the passageway as the grenades fulfill their purpose, sealing off the entrance and cutting off the spiders' pursuit.

A tense silence settles over the group as they take a moment to absorb the gravity of their actions. The soldiers exchange solemn glances, understanding the sacrifices made and the risks that still lie ahead. They gather their resolve, knowing that their mission is far from over.

With the entrance sealed, the group regroups, planning their next course of action. They understand the need to keep moving, to find a way to neutralize the spider threat once and for all. Emotions heavy and determination renewed, they brace themselves for the treacherous path that lies ahead, ready to face whatever challenges come their way as they strive to protect themselves and accomplish their mission.

General Hargrove, Dr. Stevenson, with Dr. Williams in his arms, and the remaining soldiers make their way into the main tent, their faces reflecting exhaustion and deep concern. They waste no time and immediately seek medical attention for Dr. Williams.

Inside the tent, Dr. Carter, alerted by the commotion, rushes over to assist Dr. Stevenson. Together, they work to carefully lay Dr. Williams on a medical cot, their movements precise and efficient.

"We need to assess Dr. Williams' condition immediately," Dr. Stevenson urges. "Help me lay her down." General Hargrove, joins Dr. Stevenson in positioning Dr. Williams on the cot. Their hands exhibit a delicate balance of gentleness and speed, prioritizing the injured doctor's well-being.

Dr. Ivanov, sensing the need to contribute, offers his help to the team. However, the exhaustion and tension in the air cause the others to unintentionally ignore his offer, their focus solely on attending to Dr. Williams.

Though Dr. Ivanov's assistance is temporarily overlooked, the priority remains on Dr. Williams' immediate medical assessment and care. The team concentrates on the task at hand, determined to provide the best possible support for their injured colleague.

"Dr. Ivanov, once we stabilize Dr. Williams, I would like to review our findings from down there and hear your insights on the matter," General Hargrove asserts, acknowledging the doctor's expertise.

"Of course, General," Dr. Ivanov replies promptly, his dedication evident in his response. He stands ready to provide his insights and contribute to the understanding of the situation. Meanwhile, Dr. Stevenson, requests Dr. Carter to remove Dr. Williams' blouse in order to assess the severity of the spider bites. Aware of the critical nature of their actions, Dr. Carter carefully complies, and her expression turns to shock as he witnesses the multitude of spider bites covering Dr. Williams' torso.

Drawing upon his preparedness, Dr. Stevenson retrieves a syringe and a vial of spider anti-venom from his backpack. With a mix of hope and determination, he prepares to administer the potentially life-saving treatment. "I have spider antivenom here. Let's hope it's strong enough to save her," he states, his voice laden with concern.

The race against time to counteract the venom coursing through Dr. Williams' body. With their focus on swift action, they work together to stabilize her condition and provide the necessary medical intervention, all while keeping a watchful eye on the potential long-term effects of the spider bites.

With Dr. Williams lying bare-chested, the true extent of the spider bites becomes evident, painting a grim picture of the inflicted damage. Dr. Stevenson, injects the antivenom into Dr. Williams' unconscious body. His hands exhibit a combination of precision and urgency, hoping that the treatment will prove effective.

As he administers the antidote, Dr. Stevenson's mind races with concern. He shares his thoughts, albeit with a glimmer of hope, "I'm hoping and praying that since these bites came from the juveniles, perhaps their venom is not as potent. Thank God they cannot produce acid yet. However, these bites are severe, and the venom has spread extensively."

Anticipating the need for further medical intervention, Dr. Stevenson retrieves additional supplies from his backpack. He prepares to dress the wounds, determined to minimize the damage caused by the venomous bites. Simultaneously, Dr. Carter diligently wipes the foam from Dr. Williams' mouth, ensuring her airway remains clear and unobstructed.

The team understands the critical nature of their actions and remains focused on stabilizing Dr. Williams' condition while addressing the potential complications resulting from the spider bites.

With each passing moment, they fight against time, employing their expertise and medical resources to provide the best possible care. Amidst the somber atmosphere, they cling to the hope that the combination of antivenom treatment and meticulous wound management will prove effective in saving Dr. Williams' life.

"We need to stabilize her and closely monitor her condition. Time is of the essence," Dr. Stevenson emphasizes, fully aware of the criticality of the situation. He then turns his attention to General Hargrove, seeking updates on reinforcements.

"General, any word on the reinforcements? If they haven't departed yet, we urgently require these additional medications," he says, handing over a list to the General, detailing the specific medications needed.

General Hargrove responds, "As far as I know, they are in the final stages of preparation." He immediately addresses the communication soldier, his voice firm,

"Get on the line and inform them that we have an urgent medical situation. We need those medications for one of our scientists who has been severely bitten."

Meanwhile, Dr. Carter and Dr. Stevenson work in tandem, their focus unwavering as they meticulously clean and dress Dr. Williams' wounds. Their combined expertise and determination guide their every move, aiming to minimize the risk of infection and promote the healing process.

Standing nearby, General Hargrove wears a mix of worry and hope on his face, understanding the critical importance of their actions. The remaining soldiers remain vigilant, their eyes scanning the surroundings for any potential threats that may compromise the ongoing medical operation.

Dr. Williams lies on the cot, her breathing gradually stabilizing, and her complexion showing signs of improvement. The effects of the administered antivenom are beginning to manifest, providing a glimmer of hope to Dr. Carter and Dr. Stevenson.

As they exchange a relieved glance, a sense of accomplishment washes over them. "She's stabilizing. We acted just in time," Dr. Carter acknowledges the significance of their timely intervention.

Dr. Stevenson, appreciating Dr. Carter's words, responds with gratitude, "Thank you, Doctor. Your expertise and teamwork made a difference in saving her life."

However, Dr. Stevenson remains cautiously aware of the ongoing risks. "She's not out of the woods yet," he warns. "The venom was potent, and there's a possibility of a relapse. We need additional medications to ensure her continued recovery."

General Hargrove, overhearing their conversation, "We will do whatever it takes to obtain those medications, Dr. Stevenson. Reinforcements should arrive in 12 hours, but it's going to be the longest 12 hours any of us have ever experienced."

A mix of fatigue and relief washes over the group as they begin to relax, their focus shifting to Dr. Williams' ongoing care and the anticipation of reinforcements. However, General Hargrove's attention turns to Dr. Ivanov, who stands among them, prompting curiosity about his role and potential contribution.

General Hargrove approaches Dr. Ivanov, his expression displaying a combination of expectation and inquiry. The group, weary but hopeful, awaits the doctor's response, recognizing that every individual's expertise and efforts are crucial in navigating the challenges ahead.

"Dr. Ivanov, before we reached the queen's chamber, we stumbled upon an unexpected discovery," General Hargrove begins, his tone filled with intrigue. Dr. Ivanov turns to face him, his curiosity piqued.

"What did you find, General?" Dr. Ivanov responds, his attention fully captured. The rest of the group, including Dr. Stevenson and Dr. Carter, now focused, fix their eyes on Dr. Ivanov, waiting for his reaction.

"We discovered a hidden laboratory within the cavern," General Hargrove reveals. "A laboratory filled with preserved spiders in different stages of development, accompanied by extensive scientific research documents."

Dr. Ivanov's expression wavers, a mix of surprise and unease crossing his face. He quickly responds, his voice filled with assurance, "I assure you, General, I had no knowledge of such a laboratory. It must have been kept secret by rogue scientists."

Dr. Stevenson, sensing the weight of the situation, expresses doubt, "Rogue scientists? That seems hard to believe, considering the level of sophistication and the extensive research we found."

The group becomes enveloped in a sense of intrigue and concern as they grapple with the revelation of the hidden laboratory. Questions and uncertainties abound, highlighting the need for further investigation into the origins and intentions of the mysterious scientists. The unfolding discovery adds another layer of complexity to their mission, intensifying their determination to uncover the truth and ensure the safety of all involved.

"Dr. Ivanov, can you shed some light on the purpose of these experiments? Who authorized them?" Dr. Carter presses, seeking clarification and accountability.

Dr. Ivanov hesitates, visibly uncomfortable with the line of questioning. He evades the inquiry, choosing his words carefully. "I understand your concerns, but as I mentioned before, I am as surprised as you are. This is clearly a breach of protocol."

General Hargrove, still harboring doubts, fixes his gaze firmly on Dr. Ivanov. The tension in the tent rises as everyone anxiously awaits the doctor's response, their trust in him and the Russian authorities hanging in the balance.

"Dr. Ivanov, your lack of transparency raises serious doubts about the true nature of this mission. Are you hiding something from us?" General Hargrove confronts the doctor, his voice laden with suspicion.

Dr. Ivanov, his defiance evident, stands his ground. "General Hargrove, I assure you, I am as committed to eradicating this spider threat as you are. We will get to the bottom of this, but right now, our priority should be containing the creatures."

The group finds themselves caught in a delicate and uncertain situation. Doubts and suspicions linger, casting a shadow over their collaboration. The urgency to address the immediate threat remains, but the underlying concern regarding the origins and motives of the hidden laboratory adds an additional layer of complexity.

With the commitment to containing the spider threat at the forefront, the group must navigate this newfound uncertainty, striving to maintain cohesion and trust. The road ahead becomes even more challenging as they grapple with the dual objectives of uncovering the truth behind the laboratory while ensuring the safety of themselves and the world from the mysterious spider menace.

General Hargrove, though still harboring doubts, acknowledges the immediate priority of containing the spiders. He conveys his decision, "Alright. For now, our focus remains on containing the spiders. But be aware, Dr. Ivanov, we will get to the truth eventually."

The group exchanges glances, a mixture of suspicion and determination visible in their eyes. They understand the need to maintain their collective vigilance while balancing their pressing responsibilities.

General Hargrove, Dr. Stevenson, Dr. Carter, Dr. Ivanov, and the remaining soldiers anxiously await the arrival of reinforcements, their anticipation heightened by the worsening condition of Dr. Williams. The severity of the spider bites takes a toll on her, causing great concern among the team.

With every passing moment, the realization dawns that time is rapidly slipping away. Dr. Williams' deteriorating condition serves as a stark reminder of the pressing need for immediate medical intervention and the imperative to uncover the truth behind the spider infestation.

The group stands united, driven by a shared determination to protect their colleague, unravel the mysteries surrounding the laboratory, and ultimately eliminate the spider threat. Their resolute focus intensifies as they brace themselves for the impending arrival of reinforcements, hoping that help will arrive in time to save Dr. Williams and shed light on the unsettling discoveries they have encountered.

Dr. Stevenson shares the worsening symptoms with General Hargrove. He emphasizes the critical nature of the situation, understanding that immediate medical assistance is imperative for Dr. Williams' survival.

General Hargrove reassures Dr. Stevenson,"We're doing everything we can. They are one hour out," he states, trying to provide some solace in the face of mounting desperation.

Dr. Stevenson remains steadfast by Dr. Williams' side, closely monitoring her vital signs and offering whatever comfort he can. Dr. Carter joins him, lending her continued assistance, her focus on alleviating Dr. Williams' suffering, even if momentarily.

Dr. Carter, seeking any possible solution, asks if there is anything they can do to ease Dr. Williams' symptoms. Regrettably, Dr. Stevenson responds with a heavy heart, "I'm afraid not. We can only hope that reinforcements arrive soon."

As night falls, darkness blankets the area outside the tent, intensifying the unease among the group. They are acutely aware that this is the time when the spiders have historically launched their attacks. Tension fills the air, each person on edge, bracing for any potential threat.

Suddenly, the eerie silence is shattered by the jarring sound of gunfire. The group is jolted into action, adrenaline coursing through their veins. Their training kicks in as they prepare for the imminent danger, their instincts and weapons at the ready.

The atmosphere becomes charged with a mix of fear and determination. They know that the arrival of reinforcements is imminent, but until then, they must rely on their skills, teamwork, and unwavering resolve to protect themselves, Dr. Williams, and their mission.

As the group braces for the impending danger, their worst fears become a reality. The presumed dead adult spiders, fueled by vengeance, emerge from the darkness with renewed vigor. With a menacing swarm, they converge on the main tent, their hissing and clicking piercing through the air, sending chills down the spines of those inside.

General Hargrove, demonstrating leadership in the face of adversity, issues a commanding warning to his comrades. "They're back! Brace yourselves, everyone!" His voice resounds with a mix of determination and urgency, rallying the team to prepare for the imminent confrontation.

The soldiers and remaining members of the group tighten their grips on their weapons, their senses heightened as they ready themselves for the onslaught. Fear and adrenaline surge through their veins, but their training and resilience kick in.

Inside the main tent, a tense silence settles, broken only by the haunting sounds of the approaching spiders. Each member of the group takes a deep breath, focusing their minds and stealing their nerves. They know that this battle is crucial, not only for their own survival but also for the future of their mission and the life of Dr. Williams.

As the spiders draw nearer, their presence tangible and the tension palpable, the team prepares to face the relentless swarm with every ounce of strength, skill, and determination they possess. They stand united, ready to defend themselves and push back against the encroaching threat, knowing that the outcome of this battle will shape their destiny.

Amidst the chaos outside, the soldiers scramble to defend the perimeter, unleashing a barrage of gunfire upon the swarming spiders. However, their ammunition quickly depletes, leaving them vulnerable and desperate for an alternative solution.

In a moment of panic, one soldier calls out to the General, alerting him to their dire situation. "We're out of grenades! We need something to stop them!"

The General issues a command, his voice firm and resolute. "We have to improvise! Use the fuel we have left to create fire barriers around the main tent. It's our only chance!" With swift efficiency, the group gathers fuel containers and ignites the liquid, encircling the main tent with a ring of blazing fire. The flames dance and crackle, casting an eerie glow that illuminates the darkness. The spiders, wary of the searing heat, hesitate to venture too close.

Inside the main tent, Dr. Stevenson remains steadfast at Dr. Williams' side, shielding her from the tumultuous events unfolding outside. He leans in close and whispers soothing words, his voice filled with determination and care. "Hold on, Emily. We're doing everything we can to keep you safe." Dr. Williams, her strength fading, musters a feeble smile in response, her gratitude evident despite her weakened state.

Struggling through her fever and pain, Dr. Williams musters the strength to speak. With a hint of remorse, she utters, "I'm sorry... I'm so sorry..."

Dr. Stevenson gently brushes her hair and caresses her forehead, his touch providing a sense of comfort. "Don't apologize, Emily. You fought bravely. Just hold on a little longer. Help is on the way." His words convey reassurance and unwavering support, instilling hope in the midst of darkness.

As the night wears on, the sounds of gunfire and spider hisses persist, creating an atmosphere of tension and fear. Yet, the group inside the main tent remains resolute and focused, their primary objective being the protection of Dr. Williams and their collective survival. Their determination remains unwavering as they endure the relentless onslaught, drawing strength from their unity and the unwavering belief that help will arrive in time.

As the first light of day breaks, the fire barriers surrounding the main tent prove to be effective in keeping the spiders at bay. The crackling flames create a temporary barrier, preventing the relentless creatures from advancing further. A sense of relief washes over the group, knowing that their improvised strategy has bought them some time.

Suddenly, the distinct sound of approaching helicopters pierces through the air, signaling the arrival of reinforcements. An excited soldier within the tent can't contain his joy and exclaims, "They're here! Reinforcements have arrived!"

The news spreads quickly, and the entire group is infused with renewed hope and determination. They understand that the arrival of reinforcements brings them closer to ending this harrowing ordeal.

Outside the main tent, General Hargrove and the remaining group members stand, their weariness evident, yet their spirits resilient. They shield their eyes against the blowing snow and the piercing sunlight, straining to catch a glimpse of the approaching helicopters. Anticipation fills the air as the sound grows louder, resonating in harmony with their beating hearts.

Breaking through the thick clouds, two Russian gunships and two large troop transport helicopters emerge, their presence commanding and powerful. The rotor blades slice through the air, stirring up a flurry of snowflakes, creating a whirlwind of activity. Hovering above, the helicopters create a spectacle of noise and gusts of wind that sweep through the snow-covered landscape.

Aligned in a disciplined line, the group watches with eager eyes as the helicopters descend, their skids kicking up more snow upon touchdown. The soldiers and medical personnel pour out from the aircraft, poised and ready for action. Russian and U.S.

forces join together, unified by their shared goal of containing the spider threat.

General Hargrove steps forward, greeted by the commanding officer of the Russian forces. With a firm handshake, he welcomes their counterparts. "Welcome. We have urgent matters at hand. Let's work together to end this nightmare." The Russian commander reciprocates the sentiment, expressing their commitment to support and assist. "Agreed, General. Our forces are here to provide support and assistance. Together, we will prevail."

The unity and collaboration between the two forces underscore the significance of their shared mission. With reinforcements at their side, the group finds solace in knowing that they are not alone in their fight against the encroaching spider threat. Determined and driven, they stand united, ready to face the challenges ahead and bring an end to this relentless nightmare.

With the combined forces now bolstered by the arrival of reinforcements, the group prepares for the decisive phase of their mission. The helicopters, engines humming amidst the wintry surroundings, remain parked nearby, serving as a steadfast symbol of support. Soldiers and medical personnel, driven by unwavering determination, ready themselves, ensuring their equipment is in order and their supplies are gathered.

Amidst the howling wind that whips through the main tent area, the pristine snow-covered ground serves as a stark reminder of the arduous challenges they have faced. Dr. Stevenson's eyes lift, a glimmer of relief crossing his face as he catches the sound of approaching footsteps. A Russian medical officer emerges, carrying the much-needed medicine Dr. Stevenson had requested.

A sense of gratitude washes over Dr. Stevenson as he takes hold of the medicine. The exchange between the two medical professionals transcends language barriers, as their shared commitment to saving lives unites them. Dr. Stevenson's gaze lingers for a moment, appreciating the alliance forged in the face of adversity.

The group, now further fortified by the supplies and support provided, readies themselves for the final phase of their mission. Each member, soldier and medical personnel alike, stands resolute and focused, their determination radiating in their eyes. They know that the upcoming battles will test their mettle, but they are prepared to face whatever lies ahead, unwavering in their mission to eradicate the spider threat and protect the lives of those at risk.

With the medicine secured and their resolve renewed, the group stands as a formidable force, prepared to confront the final challenges that await them. The combined strength and expertise of the American and Russian teams serve as a beacon of hope, fueling their determination to bring an end to this nightmare once and for all.

Dr. Stevenson remains steadfast at Emily's bedside, his concern evident as he strokes her hair gently. The unconscious state of his colleague weighs heavily on him, but he finds solace in the arrival of the Russian medical officer, who stands nearby, observing the scene. With expertise and precision, Dr. Stevenson administers a series of injections, each one aimed at aiding Dr. Williams' recovery. The Russian medical officer watches attentively, ready to lend assistance if needed.

Meanwhile, General Hargrove and Colonel Zhukov engage in a serious discussion away from the bustling activity of the tent, seeking a moment of privacy amidst the mission's fervor. Aware of the pressing concerns, they exchange vital information and strategies.

"So, there you have it, Colonel," General Hargrove states with a tone of gravity. "For now, we have contained the spiders. They remain inactive in the presence of sunlight or artificial light. Handguns have proven to be almost useless against them. Our best methods of combat include grenades, burning fuel, and explosives. However, we cannot underestimate their ability to dig and potentially escape through unknown access points."

The two commanders share a mutual understanding of the imminent threat posed by the spiders. They recognize the importance of covering all known access points to prevent any further escape attempts. The weight of the mission and the lives at stake hangs in the air, intensifying the seriousness of their conversation.

Amidst the activity within the tent, the General and the Colonel stand united, their minds focused on devising effective strategies to neutralize the spider threat once and for all. Their collaboration serves as a testament to the joint efforts of the American and Russian forces, highlighting the shared determination to overcome this nightmare and safeguard humanity.

As the discussion continues, the bustling atmosphere of the tent persists. Each member of the group plays their part, driven by a sense of purpose and a commitment to the mission. The hours ahead will test their strength, resilience, and resourcefulness, but with their combined expertise and determination, they remain poised to face the challenges that lie ahead.

Colonel Zhukov's attentive demeanor showcases his understanding of the seriousness of the situation. He acknowledges General Hargrove's instructions, fully committed to prioritizing the deployment of resources and providing assistance to neutralize the spider threat effectively. The shared determination between the two commanders serves as a powerful testament to their unified mission.

Meanwhile, General Hargrove moves into the medical area of the main tent, where Dr. Stevenson diligently tends to the patients. He approaches Dr. Emily Williams, who lies on a bed, in the midst of her recovery. Concern etches the General's face as he inquires about her condition.

Dr. Stevenson meets the General's gaze, offering a glimmer of optimism in his response. "She's taken a turn for the better, General. Her vitals have stabilized, and her fever is gone. It was touch and go for a little while, but she's showing signs of improvement." The weight of worry that had burdened General Hargrove's features begins to ease, replaced by a palpable sense of relief.

In that moment, the bond between commander and soldier transcends their respective roles. General Hargrove's genuine concern for Dr. Williams is evident, reflecting the deep trust and camaraderie that has developed within their team. The news of her progress offers a renewed sense of hope, bolstering their resolve to see the mission through to a successful conclusion.

With their shared dedication to the well-being of their team members and the ultimate goal of eradicating the spider threat, General Hargrove and

Dr. Stevenson stand united. The combined efforts of the American and Russian forces, working hand in hand, serve as a beacon of hope amidst the darkness. Their determination remains unyielding as they forge ahead, ready to face whatever challenges lie ahead, bolstered by the positive news of Dr. Williams' recovery.

Dr. Ivanov's presence interrupts the conversation between Dr. Stevenson and General Hargrove. The tension in the air is palpable as he seeks a moment of the General's time. Dr. Stevenson starts to excuse himself, but the General insists that he stays, indicating that whatever Dr. Ivanov has to say is relevant for everyone involved.

With a composed demeanor, Dr. Ivanov addresses General Hargrove, acknowledging the lingering doubts that exist regarding his previous claims. He speaks with sincerity, his voice carrying a mix of understanding and earnestness. "General, I understand that you still do not trust me when I said I had no knowledge about the secret lab in the borehole," Dr. Ivanov states, acknowledging the skepticism that surrounds him.

Dr. Stevenson and General Hargrove exchange glances, their curiosity piqued. They listen intently, giving Dr. Ivanov an opportunity to explain his perspective.

"I assure you, General, that I was unaware of the existence of the lab and the rogue scientists conducting unauthorized experiments. My intention was solely to aid in eliminating the spider threat and ensure the safety of everyone involved," Dr. Ivanov explains, emphasizing his commitment to the mission.

There is a pause as the weight of Dr. Ivanov's words hangs in the air. General Hargrove considers his response, contemplating the information he has received thus far. The atmosphere is charged with anticipation, waiting for the General's decision on how to proceed.

After a moment of contemplation, General Hargrove speaks, his tone firm yet open to the possibility of resolution. "Dr. Ivanov, trust is not easily earned, but it can be regained through actions. Your cooperation moving forward will be closely monitored, and your commitment to the mission will be thoroughly evaluated. We will get to the truth behind the secret lab, and those responsible will be held accountable. Until then, our priority remains the safety of our team and the eradication of the spider threat."

Dr. Ivanov nods, understanding the General's position. He accepts the scrutiny placed upon him and remains determined to prove his dedication to the mission and regain the trust that has been fractured.

With the conversation concluded, the group remains focused on their shared objective. The mission at hand transcends individual concerns, and the unity among the team remains paramount as they navigate the challenges ahead.

General Hargrove listens attentively to Dr. Ivanov's plea, his skepticism gradually giving way to a sense of understanding. Dr. Ivanov's urgency and determination to uncover the truth resonate with him, and he realizes the importance of obtaining concrete evidence to support their claims.

"I understand your position, Dr. Ivanov," General Hargrove acknowledges, his tone more receptive. "Collecting concrete evidence would indeed lend credibility to our claims. However, re-entering the borehole is a significant undertaking and comes with its own risks."

Dr. Ivanov seizes the opportunity to emphasize the necessity of their mission. "Exactly, General. If we can obtain visual documentation of the lab and the spider specimens, it would greatly strengthen our case. We need irrefutable evidence that will force our governments to address the truth behind these experiments."

General Hargrove contemplates the proposition, recognizing the potential impact such evidence could have. The weight of their shared responsibility settles upon him as he realizes the significance of their task in unveiling the truth.

"Dr. Ivanov, I understand the gravity of what you're suggesting," the General responds, his voice tinged with a mix of caution and determination. "Re-entering the borehole poses risks, but the pursuit of truth and justice sometimes demands great sacrifices. If we can gather the evidence needed to expose the secret laboratory, it may serve as a catalyst for the necessary actions to be taken."

The two men exchange a meaningful glance, their shared determination solidifying their resolve. They understand that the path ahead will not be easy, but their commitment to the mission and the safety of their teams remains unwavering.

General Hargrove takes a deep breath, making a decision. "Dr. Ivanov, we will explore the possibility of re-entering the borehole and collecting the evidence needed. But we must prioritize the safety of our teams and ensure that we have the necessary resources and support in place. This will require careful planning and coordination between our governments. The truth must be brought to light, but not at the cost of further endangering our teams."

Dr. Ivanov nods in agreement, acknowledging the need for meticulous planning and collaboration. The weight of their task hangs heavy in the air, but with their shared determination and the newfound understanding between them, they embark on a path that may unveil the secrets hidden within the depths of the Kola borehole.

General Hargrove and Colonel Zhukov sit at a table, their focus fixated on the drawings and plans of the borehole. Their discussion underscores the importance of careful planning and coordination for the upcoming mission. The truth behind the secret laboratory and the spider threat hangs heavy in the air, driving their determination.

As they engage in a focused conversation, General Hargrove and Colonel Zhukov delve into the details of the operation. They weigh the resources and manpower required, considering the potential risks and challenges that lie ahead.

"Colonel, we must carefully consider the resources and personnel needed for this operation," General Hargrove asserts, his tone earnest. "The existence of the secret laboratory and the persistent threat posed by the spiders demand our utmost preparedness."

Colonel Zhukov nods in agreement, fully aware of the seriousness of the situation. "Indeed, General. We cannot afford any oversights. Sufficient manpower and equipment must be in place to handle any unforeseen circumstances." Together, they examine the plans and drawings, their minds working in unison to formulate a strategy that maximizes their chances of success.

"I propose that we deploy a combined force of U.S. and Russian soldiers," General Hargrove suggests, his voice conveying a sense of determination. "Equipped with flamethrowers and a generous supply of grenades, our soldiers can lead the way, effectively neutralizing the spiders with the flamethrowers, while the grenades provide additional firepower."

Colonel Zhukov considers the suggestion carefully, weighing the potential benefits of such an approach. After a moment of contemplation, he meets General Hargrove's gaze and responds resolutely, "Agreed, General."

With a series of commands in Russian, Colonel Zhukov sets his troops into motion, ensuring they are armed with grenades and flamethrowers. The room fills with purposeful activity as soldiers prepare for the upcoming mission. General Hargrove and Colonel Zhukov exchange determined looks, their shared commitment evident in their eyes.

"Very well, Colonel," General Hargrove states firmly. "We will re-enter the borehole in 10 minutes. Time is of the essence, and together, we will unveil the truth and eliminate the spider threat once and for all."

The room buzzes with focused energy as the joint U.S. and Russian forces prepare to embark on their mission. The weight of their shared responsibility hangs in the air, but the determination and collaboration between the two commanders give them hope that they will prevail.

General Hargrove and Colonel Zhukov stand before the imposing entrance to the top-secret laboratory deep within the borehole. The intense battle against the spiders has brought them to this critical moment. They are accompanied by their dedicated soldiers, armed with flamethrowers and grenades, ready to defend their position.

As the soldiers prepare their equipment, the swarm of angry spiders emerges from the darkness, crawling towards them with menacing intent. The soldiers quickly react, unleashing torrents of fire from their flamethrowers, engulfing the spiders in flames. The soldiers stand resolute, driving the creatures back with a fierce determination.

Amidst the chaos and the screeching of the spiders, General Hargrove and Colonel Zhukov lead the way, their bravery inspiring their troops. The soldiers form a protective circle around them, their flamethrowers blazing, keeping the relentless arachnids at bay.

They navigate through the treacherous tunnels, encountering more spiders along the way. The battle continues, with well-placed grenades causing explosions that momentarily disorient and scatter the spiders. The soldiers press forward, their resolve unyielding.

Finally, they reach the massive metal door, the entrance to the long-hidden laboratory. The soldiers form a defensive line, holding off the relentless spider assault as General Hargrove and Colonel Zhukov approach the door.

"This is it," General Hargrove declares, his voice filled with determination. He turns to Colonel Zhukov, their shared goal of gathering evidence in mind. "We should document this discovery. Let's take pictures and videos to provide irrefutable proof."

Colonel Zhukov nods, recognizing the importance of capturing visual evidence. He signals a Russian soldier to start recording the entrance to the lab, ensuring that their efforts to expose the truth will not go unnoticed.

With cameras rolling and photographs taken, General Hargrove and Colonel Zhukov stand before the entrance, aware that the evidence they gather will play a crucial role in bringing the hidden secrets to light. They exchange a determined look, united in their purpose and ready to uncover the truth behind the secret laboratory.

General Hargrove and Colonel Zhukov lead the soldiers into the mysterious laboratory, their senses heightened and their flamethrowers at the ready. As they step inside, the heavy door shuts behind them, cutting off the outside world. The distant sounds of hissing and clicking mandibles serve as a chilling reminder of the lurking danger outside.

Two soldiers take up their positions by the door, keeping a watchful eye for any potential spider threats. Inside the dimly lit lab, the soldiers are greeted by a sprawling maze of shelves, workstations, and glass enclosures. The scene before them leaves them in awe and disbelief.

Rows upon rows of large vials line the shelves, each containing spiders in different stages of development. Some vials hold fully grown adult spiders, while others house delicate spider eggs and tiny juvenile specimens. The sheer magnitude of the collection is overwhelming.

Scientific documentation and research papers are scattered throughout the lab, offering insights into the experiments, genetic studies, and behavioral observations conducted on the spiders. The soldiers realize the magnitude of the discoveries they have made. General Hargrove, recognizing the importance of documenting the evidence, instructs one soldier to continue recording video, focusing on the spider specimens. To another soldier, he assigns the task of photographing the documents, emphasizing the need to collect as much hardcopy as possible.

Colonel Zhukov follows suit, directing his soldiers to gather evidence and document the laboratory's contents. General Hargrove, his expression a mix of concern and determination, walks towards a large computer monitor at a nearby workstation. The monitor displays a wealth of notes and calculations, capturing his attention. He studies the information carefully, striving to comprehend the depths of the scientific research conducted within these walls.

The soldiers, surrounded by the eerie presence of the spiders and immersed in a labyrinth of scientific discovery, stand in silent awe. The weight of the truth they are uncovering and the responsibility to expose it hangs heavily in the air.

With the charges set and the preparations complete, the soldiers gather around General Hargrove and Colonel Zhukov, ready to execute the plan. The setting sun casts an orange glow over the landscape, creating an atmosphere of anticipation.

General Hargrove addresses the group, his voice firm and resolute. “We have a limited window of opportunity to carry out this operation. Once the charges are detonated, we must retreat to a safe distance. Our objective is to collapse the tunnels and seal off the borehole, preventing the spiders from escaping and causing further harm.”

Colonel Zhukov translates the general’s words to the Russian soldiers, ensuring clear communication and unity in their mission. The soldiers exchange determined glances, their faces etched with a combination of courage and concern.

General Hargrove looks at Colonel Zhukov, their eyes conveying mutual understanding and trust. “Colonel, let’s do this together. Once the charges are detonated, we regroup and secure the perimeter. Our combined forces will ensure that no spider makes it out alive.”

The soldiers tighten their grips on their weapons, their hearts pounding with anticipation. With a nod from General Hargrove, the command is given, and the charges are remotely detonated. A thunderous explosion rips through the air, sending shockwaves reverberating through the caverns.

Dust and debris fill the air as the tunnels collapse, sealing off the borehole. The ground trembles beneath their feet, a testament to the power of their actions. The soldiers retreat to a safe distance, their eyes fixed on the site, ensuring the success of their mission.

As the dust settles and the silence descends upon the scene, a collective sense of accomplishment and relief washes over the group. They have taken a significant step towards neutralizing the spider threat, safeguarding the world from its deadly reach.

General Hargrove and Colonel Zhukov exchange a knowing glance, acknowledging the magnitude of their joint effort. The soldiers, weary but filled with a renewed sense of purpose, regroup and reinforce the perimeter, ensuring that no spider escapes the confines of the collapsed tunnels.

The battle is not over, but this decisive action has bought them time to strategize and plan for the next phase. With their unified forces, General Hargrove, Colonel Zhukov, and their soldiers stand ready to face whatever challenges lie ahead in their mission to eliminate the spider menace once and for all.

The ground beneath them begins to crack open, revealing a massive chasm that stretches out before them. The soldiers and leaders scramble to maintain their balance, their expressions filled with shock and disbelief. From the depths of the newly formed abyss, an unimaginable number of spiders emerge, their legs skittering and their eyes gleaming with malice.

Fear grips the soldiers as they witness the overwhelming force of the spider horde. General Hargrove and Colonel Zhukov exchange a glance, their faces grim with the realization that their previous actions may have only exacerbated the situation. They know that they must find a way to confront this unprecedented threat head-on.

With quick thinking, General Hargrove commands the soldiers to regroup and form a defensive line. They tighten their grip on their weapons, readying themselves for a battle unlike any they have faced before. Flames erupt from the flamethrowers as the soldiers unleash a torrent of fire, pushing back the relentless advance of the spiders.

But the sheer numbers of the spider swarm are overwhelming. The soldiers fight valiantly, their hearts filled with determination, but they are quickly becoming outnumbered. Venomous fangs and razor-sharp legs lash out, leaving wounds and casualties in their wake.

Dr. Stevenson and Dr. Carter, their medical expertise pushed to the limit, work tirelessly to treat the injured soldiers. Their hands move with precision, administering life-saving treatments amidst the chaos of the battle. Every second counts as they fight to stabilize the wounded and keep them in the fight.

General Hargrove and Colonel Zhukov, their leadership tested once again, strategize on the fly, searching for any weakness or vulnerability in the spider swarm. They coordinate the soldiers' movements, directing their firepower with precision, aiming to disrupt the spiders' coordinated assault.

The battle rages on, the clash between humanity and the spider horde intensifying with each passing moment. The soldiers fight with unwavering resolve, their determination fueled by the need to protect one another and to preserve the safety of the world beyond.

Amidst the chaos, a glimmer of hope emerges. Dr. Stevenson, in a moment of inspiration, formulates a plan to exploit the spiders' weakness. He shares his idea with General Hargrove and Colonel Zhukov, their eyes widening with a renewed sense of possibility. Together, they rally the soldiers, shifting their tactics and focusing their efforts on a concentrated assault. With synchronized precision, the soldiers create a diversion, drawing the attention of the spiders while a small, specialized team maneuvers to strike at the heart of the spider horde.

Explosions rock the battlefield as the soldiers detonate carefully placed charges, creating a cascade of chaos within the spider swarm. The ground trembles, and the spiders falter, their advance momentarily disrupted. It is a fleeting opportunity, but one that the soldiers seize with all their might.

In a concerted effort, the soldiers unleash a torrent of firepower, targeting the weakened areas of the spider horde. Flames roar and bullets pierce the air, pushing back the spiders with a relentless determination. The soldiers fight with every ounce of strength, refusing to yield to the overwhelming force that seeks to engulf them.

Slowly but steadily, the tide of battle turns. The spiders retreat, their numbers dwindling as the soldiers regain control of the battlefield. The determination and resilience of the soldiers, coupled with their unwavering unity, prove to be the turning point in this desperate struggle.

Exhausted but victorious, the soldiers regroup, their bodies covered in grime and their spirits worn but unbroken. They tend to the wounded, offering support and solace to their fallen comrades. General Hargrove and Colonel Zhukov exchange a nod, their shared understanding of the sacrifices made and the resilience shown in the face of unimaginable odds.

As the dust settles, a sense of calm descends upon the battlefield. The soldiers take a moment to catch their breath, their eyes scanning the area for any signs of further threat. Though the battle is won, they remain vigilant, knowing that the spider menace may still linger.

General Hargrove, Colonel Zhukov, Dr. Stevenson, Dr. Carter, and the soldiers stand together, their faces etched with a mix of exhaustion and triumph. They have faced the unimaginable, and through their unwavering determination, they have emerged victorious.

Suddenly, out of one of the cave-like openings a good distance from the borehole, an explosion takes place blowing a considerable amount of the terrain away.

As the dust settles, the soldiers slowly rise to their feet, their eyes widening in horror as a colossal creature emerges from the smoldering wreckage of the borehole. "My God... it's the queen!"

The gargantuan arachnid with massive legs and a ferocious demeanor slowly climbs out of the cave. Her eyes gleam with anger as she surveys the scene, her presence commanding and intimidating. A stunned

General Hargrove looks on. "How... how did she survive the explosion?"

General Hargrove and Colonel Zhukov exchange grim looks, realizing the magnitude of the threat they now face. "Enough is enough," a determined General Hargrove says. "We cannot let her escape. We must bring this bitch down before she wreaks havoc on the world."

Colonel Zhukov shouts an order to two soldiers who run to one of the helicopters. They return with two rocket launchers and await orders from Colonel Zhukov. As the queen advances, her massive legs pound the ground, causing tremors with each step. The soldiers with flamethrowers unleash a stream of deadly flame, but the queen becomes even more angry and spews deadly acid at the soldiers knocking them to the ground in agony.

Observing this, Dr. Stevenson shouts to Dr. Carter. "Doctor Carter, follow me. He grabs his medical kit and the two rush to give aid to the injured Russian soldiers avoiding the queen's acid spray.

The soldiers unleash a relentless assault, launching grenades, and coordinating attacks to bring down the queen spider. More flamethrowers roar to life, engulfing the creature in a sea of fire. The queen retaliates, swiping with her gigantic legs, causing havoc among the soldiers. The ground shakes beneath their feet, and they fight valiantly, determined not to let her advance.

Explosions continue to rock the battlefield as the soldiers fight desperately to weaken the queen spider's defenses. The deafening screeches and hisses of the queen echo through the air, disorienting the soldiers.

Colonel Zhukov, straining to be heard, yells to his troops. "Soldiers! Focus your fire! We must bring down the queen!" Despite their efforts, more soldiers sustain injuries as they relentlessly press on. The two Russians soldiers that had the rocket launchers are attacked by the queen who spews acid on them. They roll on the ground in agony. "General, if we can reach my men with the rocket launchers, we might have a chance."

General Hargrove scans the terrain between them and the soldiers equipped with rocket launchers. The queen's massive form looms between them, creating an obstacle they must overcome. "Let's make a run for it. We'll circle around the queen to reach them." The two officers take off, their hearts pounding as they dodge the queen's attacks. They alternate throwing grenades, forcing the queen to retreat momentarily, buying them precious time. They manage to reach the badly injured soldiers and retrieve the two rocket launchers, their hands shaking with anticipation.

"I'll aim for her head. You take a shot at her abdomen. Good luck, Colonel."

The two officers focus their attention on their shots. General Hargrove steadies himself, takes aim, and fires his rocket launcher. The projectile strikes the queen's mouth, causing her to stagger backward in pain.

"Now, it's my turn!" the Colonel said. Colonel Zhukov takes careful aim and launches his rocket, hitting the queen squarely in the abdomen. The explosion ruptures the giant arachnid, releasing a yellowish, horrid-smelling liquid. The queen emits a blood-curdling screech, her legs convulsing before she pulls them tightly to her body, succumbing to her wounds. The soldiers, witnessing the demise of the queen, pause for a moment, their hearts filled with relief and awe.

"We did it. We defeated the queen," General Hargrove, breathing heavily, exclaims.

Solemnly Colonel Zhukov nodding adds, "It's over... for now." The soldiers cheer, their battle cries mingling with the dissipating echoes of the queen's screeches.

In the main tent, Russian medical staff and Dr. Stevenson rush to tend to the wounded soldiers. General Hargrove and Colonel Zhukov, exhausted but triumphant, exchange a nod of mutual respect. General Hargrove turns to the Colonel. "We've won this battle, but we must remain vigilant. There may be more out there."

"I agree General. I will make sure all the openings are still monitored." The soldiers gather their fallen comrades, paying homage to their sacrifice. They begin the arduous task of regrouping and fortifying their defenses, knowing that their fight against the spider menace might not be over.

Before the American team leaves the borehole site, General Hargrove and the Colonel discuss how to contain the area until the Russian authorities can come up with a final solution in case somehow, other creatures from beneath decide to emerge. The two commanders shake hands before one of the copters takeoff with the American contingent.

Two months later, Dr. Williams was glad to be back at Duke University. Her spider bites had healed, and she and Dr. Stevenson were now an item. She stood confidently at the podium, preparing to address her graduate students. The lecture hall was filled with eager students, ready to absorb her knowledge.

"Today, we were fortunate enough to have Dr. Carter, a renowned volcanologist who recently returned from Italy and Mt. Vesuvius. I believe she has some valuable information to share with all of you from her recent visit to the famous volcano. Dr. Carter steps forward, prepared to take over the lecture.

"Thank you, Dr. Williams. It's an honor to be here at this prestigious university and share my recent findings with you on the former and recent volcanic activity on Mt. Vesuvius." Just as Dr. Carter is about to start her lecture, the lecture hall doors swing open, drawing everyone's attention. Three familiar federal agents walk in, capturing the room's attention.

The same female agent that whisked Dr. Williams away to the Kola Superdeep Borehole walks towards the stage with her two male associates. "Dr. Williams, Dr. Carter, we have urgent news. There has been an eruption at the Project Mohole dig site. You both need to come with us immediately."

TRIBUTE
TO THE MOVIE POSTERS
OF CREATURE FILMS
OF THE PAST

CREATURE FROM THE BLACK LAGOON
Starring
RICHARD CARLSON · JULIA ADAMS
RICHARD DENNING · ANTONIO MORENO · NESTOR PAIVA · WHIT BISSELL
DIRECTED BY JACK ARNOLD · SCREENPLAY BY HARRY ESSEX AND ARTHUR ROSS · PRODUCED BY WILLIAM ALLAND · A UNIVERSAL-INTERNATIONAL PICTURE

STARRING
STEVE McQUEEN
IN
THE BLOB
INDESCRIBABLE...
INDESTRUCTIBLE!
NOTHING CAN STOP IT!
AND CO STARRING
ANETA CORSEAUT
EARL ROWE
COLONIAL
MIDNIGHT SPOOK SHOW
DAUGHTER OF HORROR
BELA LUGOSI
Healthfully AIR CONDITIONED
PRODUCED BY JACK H. HARRIS
DIRECTED BY IRVIN S. YEAWORTH, JR.
SCREENPLAY BY THEODORE SIMONSON AND KATE PHILLIPS
IRVINE H. MILLGATE
NONSTOP ENTERTAINMENT
A TONYLYN PRODUCTION

ARCHIVE COLLECTION
A HORROR HORDE OF CRAWL-AND-CRUSH GIANTS
CLAWING OUT OF THE EARTH
FROM MILE-DEEP
CATACOMBS!
THEM

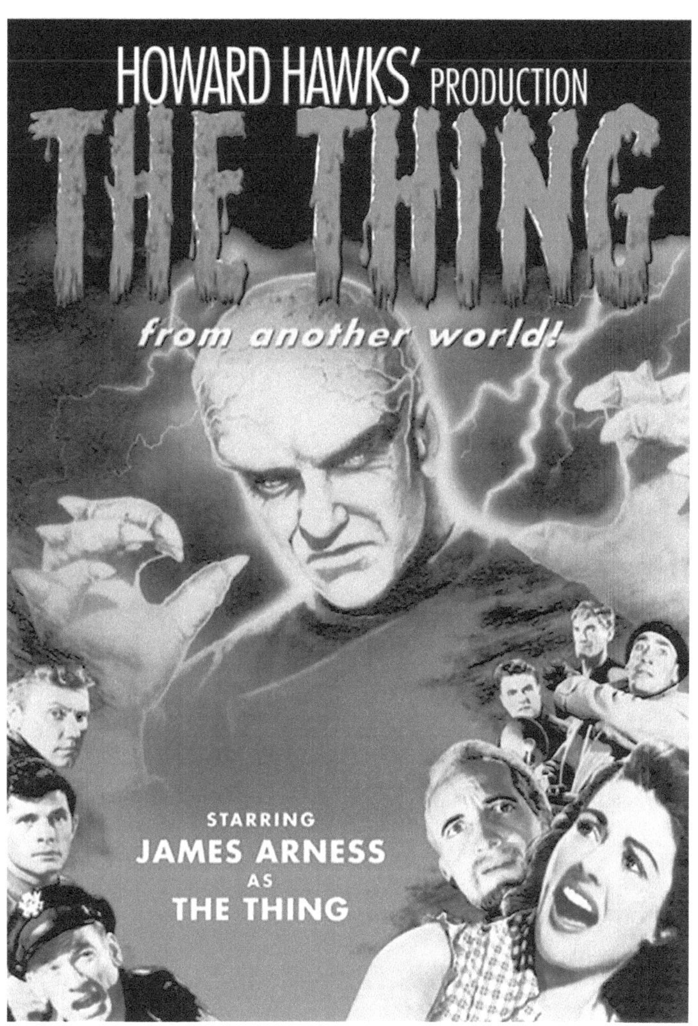
HOWARD HAWKS' PRODUCTION
THE THING
from another world!
STARRING
JAMES ARNESS
AS
THE THING

AT THIS VERY MOMENT SPACE SHIPS FROM THE BEYOND MAY BE ON THEIR WAY TO DESTROY OUR PLANET!
H. G. WELLS'
The
War of the Worlds
GENE BARRY · ANN ROBINSON
GEORGE PAL
BYRON HASKIN
BARRE LYNDON
TECHNICOLOR

INCREDIBLE, UNSTOPPABLE TITAN OF TERROR!
GODZILLA
It's Alive!
KING OF THE MONSTERS!
CIVILIZATION CRUMBLES as its death rays blast a city of 6 million from the face of the earth!
RAYMOND BURR
MIGHTIEST MONSTER!
MIGHTIEST MELODRAMA of them all!

RKO
DAVID O. SELZNICK
Executive Producer
KING KONG
with
FAY WRAY ◇ ROBT. ARMSTRONG
BRUCE CABOT
A COOPER-SCHOEDSACK PRODUCTION
FROM AN IDEA CONCEIVED BY
EDGAR WALLACE AND MERIAN C. COOPER

THUNDERING OUT OF
UNKNOWN SKIES–
The Super-Sonic Hell-Creature
No Weapon Could Destroy!
THE FLYING MONSTER...
RODAN
THE KING BROTHERS
present A TOHO PRODUCTION
DCA
print by TECHNICOLOR

MIGHTIEST MONSTER IN ALL CREATION!
RAVISHING A UNIVERSE FOR LOVE!
MOTHRA
TOHOSCOPE
EASTMAN
COLOR
Screenplay by SHINICHI SEKIZAWA
Produced by TOMOYUKI TANAKA
Directed by INOSHIRO HONDA
Special Effects by EIJI TSUBURAYA
A TOHO PRODUCTION
A COLUMBIA PICTURES RELEASE

THE BLACK SCORPION
DON'T BE ASHAMED TO SCREAM –
IT HELPS TO RELIEVE THE TENSION.

GIANT SPIDER STRIKES!
..CRAWLING TERROR 100 FEET HIGH!
Universal-International presents
TARANTULA!
STARRING
JOHN AGAR
MARA CORDAY
LEO G. CARROLL
with NESTOR PAIVA · ROSS ELLIOTT

FROM OUT OF SPACE....
A WARNING AND AN ULTIMATUM!
THE DAY THE EARTH STOOD STILL
WITH
MICHAEL RENNIE · PATRICIA NEAL · HUGH MARLOWE
SAM JAFFE · BILLY GRAY · FRANCES BAVIER · LOCK MARTIN
JULIAN BLAUSTEIN · ROBERT WISE · EDMUND H. NORTH
20th CENTURY-FOX

BEWARE THE TRIFFIDS... they grow
...know...walk...talk...stalk...and KILL!
THE DAY OF THE TRIFFIDS
From the greatest
science-fiction novel
of all time!
THE DAY OF THE TRIFFIDS
IN CINEMASCOPE AND EASTMANCOLOR
STARRING
HOWARD KEEL
NICOLE MAUREY
Executive Producer PHILIP YORDAN · Produced by GEORGE PITCHER · Directed by STEVE SEKELY · Screenplay by PHILIP YORDAN
From the Novel by JOHN WYNDHAM
Author of "VILLAGE OF THE DAMNED"
A SECURITY PICTURES LTD. PRODUCTION
AN ALLIED ARTISTS RELEASE

DELUXE WIDESCREEN PRESENTATION
The Tingler
Spine-"Tingling"
40th
ANNIVERSARY
Presentation
DVD
VIDEO

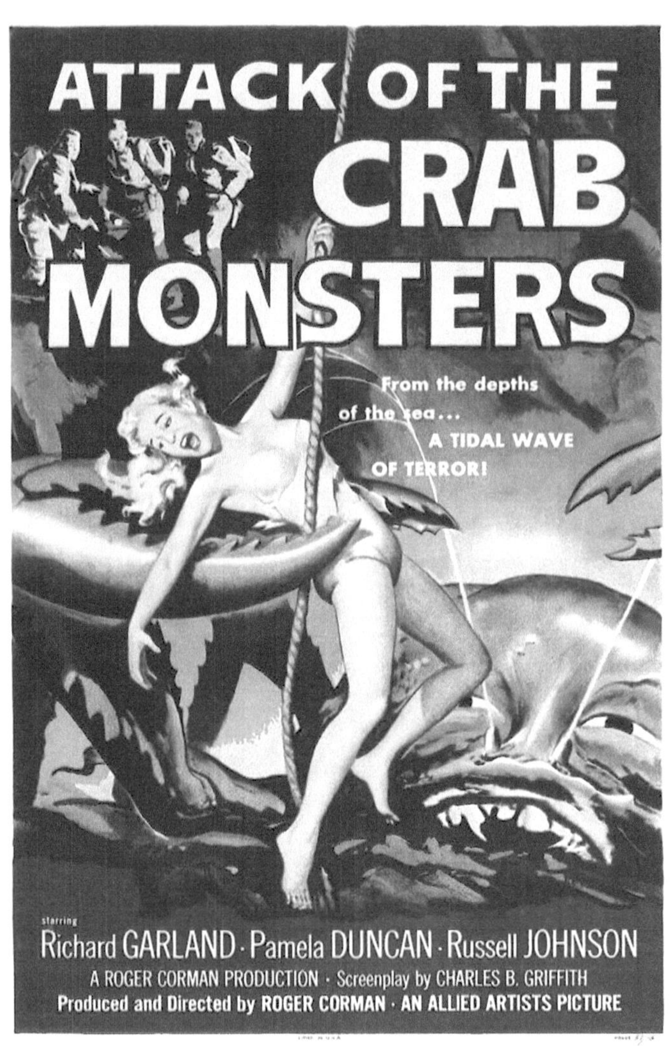
ATTACK OF THE
CRAB
MONSTERS
From the depths
of the sea...
A TIDAL WAVE
OF TERROR!
starring
Richard GARLAND · Pamela DUNCAN · Russell JOHNSON
A ROGER CORMAN PRODUCTION · Screenplay by CHARLES B. GRIFFITH
Produced and Directed by ROGER CORMAN · AN ALLIED ARTISTS PICTURE

THEY COULDN'T BELIEVE THEIR EYES!
THEY COULDN'T ESCAPE THE TERROR!
AND NEITHER WILL YOU!
THE SEA'S MASTER-BEAST OF THE AGES–RAGING UP FROM THE BOTTOM OF TIME!
"It's alive!"
WARNER BROS. PRESENT
"The Beast From 20,000 Fathoms"
YOU'LL SEE IT TEAR A CITY APART!
CAST OF THOUSANDS! OVER A YEAR IN THE MAKING!
PAUL CHRISTIAN · PAULA RAYMOND · CECIL KELLAWAY · KENNETH TOBEY · JACK PENNICK
LOU MORHEIM · FRED FREIBERGER
Suggested by the Sensational SATURDAY EVENING POST Story by RAY BRADBURY
HAL CHESTER · JACK DIETZ · EUGENE LOURIE
WARNER BROS.

OTHER BOOKS BY THE AUTHOR

JEANNIE LOOMIS THRILLER NOVELS

Ark of the Covenant – Raid on the Church of Our Lady Mary of Axion

Star Chamber

Time Game

Rollercoaster

The Fourth Reich

House of Special Purpose

The Phantom Train

Black Heart/Black Cell

Forgotten Plans

Thin Blue Line

HORROR NOVELS

House on Haunted Hill Resurrection

NON-FICTION

Towards the Integration of Police Psychological Techniques to Combat K-12 Juvenile Delinquency

Hitting Rock Bottom (Amazon Best-seller)

Teaching Behind the Walls

How to Create a Public-School Military Style Boot Camp

www.ingramcontent.com/pod-product-compliance
Lightning Source LLC
Chambersburg PA
CBHW020550310726
48979CB00008B/1155/J

* 9 7 9 8 9 8 8 6 8 2 3 2 5 *